Also by Sage Webb

The Unremarkable Circumstances of Inmate 17656-090
The Venturi Effect*

*Forthcoming Stoneman House Press November 2020

L*ve & Other Misunderstandings

L*ve & Other Misunderstandings

SAGE WEBB

STONEMAN HOUSE PRESS, L.L.C.
HOUSTON

www.stonemanhouse.com

L*ve & Other Misunderstandings

Copyright © 2020 Sage Webb
All rights reserved, including the right of reproduction, in whole or in part, in any form.

Paperback ISBN 978-1-7337379-0-6
Ebook ISBN 978-1-7337379-2-0

Published in the United States of America by Stoneman House Press, L.L.C. 2020

The stories here are all works of fiction. Names, characters, and incidents are the products of the author's imagination. In the case of real places, these locales are used in a fictitious manner. Any resemblance to actual people or events is unintended and completely coincidental.

Jacket photos © Warren Talley and SL Pro Solutions, L.L.C.
All rights reserved. Used with permission.

STONEMAN HOUSE PRESS, L.L.C.
Houston, TX
U.S.A.
www.stonemanhouse.com

To Bob and Beverly
and to 'Sheda
and to Virgil

Thank you all for dancing . . . always dancing. . . .

Contents

Contents

Contents

Contents

Francis Roy Winters, Esq., Dives Off a Dock

Mr. Frank Winters had tight curls, rings of coarse hair bleached white by age and stress, hair that matched the coats of the Bichon Frises the often-unsober Mrs. Hanes would parade on the yacht-club lawn while wearing too-tight yoga pants with a pink thong poking over the pants' strained waistband. On Friday evenings, Mr. Winters would order Negronis with extra vermouth, and even though I got my tips from an automatic 18.5% service charge added to every chit, he would put a fifty-dollar bill under his last empty glass before carrying his at-least two hundred fifty pounds down the curving front stairway of the yacht club at the end of the night. Mostly Mr. Winters talked about his boat, a mahogany Grand Banks 36 trawler—the oldest Grand Banks on the Gulf Coast. He would tell the other club members in the bar about the new inverter he'd had installed or the new saloon paint Jorge Gutierrez was applying to "spruce the old girl up."

Only occasionally, and only after more than two Negronis, Mr. Winters would talk about his cases. Usually, he talked to Mr. Cardenas and Mr. Charles, but I'd heard him talk a little with Mrs. Ulibarri, who was new to the club and had practiced criminal law in New Mexico before moving to Houston. If none of those attorneys were around, which was more often the case after eleven p.m. than before, Mr. Winters would move from the heavy beech table by the tall windows overlooking the pool and harbor and reseat himself at the bar and ask how the night had been for me. I would reply honestly: "busy, and sometimes when it gets like that, it's hard to keep everyone happy," or "the kitchen fouled up every appetizer order I sent back," in which case I'd frown and he'd nod. And then he'd tell me about his day.

Mr. Winters never gave specifics. At the time, I didn't understand attorney-client privilege and confidences and all that. I do now (Mr.

Winters, in fact, is probably the biggest reason I ended up in law school), but back then, all those things dwelled in an ether of which I was unaware. What Mr. Winters did give was what he called "the shattered idyll of the esquire." He told me how a high LSAT score lifted him from the poverty of an Indiana farm, a family operation sustained by a mother widowed by a combine accident a month before Mr. Winters's birth. The score got him into the University of Chicago, a school from which he could have gone just about anywhere, he said. But he went to the Cook County Public Defender's Office to "fight for the tired, the poor, the huddled masses yearning to breathe free, or something like that," as he put it.

The night he told me about moving to Texas, at the urging of his first wife, who had grown up on Galveston, I think he teared up. I remember the way he stared through me, through the back wall of Ron Zacapa and Remy Martin XO and other bottles, glass soldiers of amber and saffron and turquoise . . . and some colorless. He told me of his excitement at leaving the public defender's and striking out on his own, and with no hint of pomp, he told me how he'd built a multi-million-dollar practice of partners and associates in Houston and Corpus and San Antonio and Dallas.

That night, there was a story about defending a senator charged with tax and wire fraud, and one about an oil mogul with a propensity for women problems and hallucinogens. Before he slipped the $50 under the last empty glass, he told me he was going to apply to take what he called court-appointed cases, to "get back to his roots," he said. He said federal courts gave private counsel these court-appointed cases when the public defender's office couldn't take them, and he said he wanted to get on the list of attorneys who accepted such work. And I guess he did—get on the list—because he dove off the dock about a year and a half later.

The night of the dive, a group of club members who fancied themselves musicians was playing on the deck outside the club bar, strumming guitars and wailing "Margaritaville" and "Southern Cross." This group would gather every couple weeks for these unpracticed performances and everyone would compete to run my kegs dry. The club would put out free pizza and pot stickers and a silver platter of vegetables that no one touched and which, afterward, Graciela from the kitchen would take home for her kids' lunches. That night progressed like most other such affairs, except Mr. Winters only ordered one Negroni and sat by himself inside the bar, watching the fête on the patio through the french doors I'd squeegeed clean earlier that day.

"How's life, Mr. W?" I asked.

"I buried another of my selves today," he said, "but I can't seem to laugh tonight."

He didn't turn away from the glass doors when he said it. The sun had set and the doors had started to act more as mirrors than windows, but one could still see Mrs. Hanes as she crouched in front of the band and then pushed herself up into one of the yoga headstands she loved to perform at functions. Her shirt slipped down around her chin, and even with the reflections on the glass and the distance, I could see the train wreck of dark bra cups heaving in and out.

Mr. Winters snorted. "I can't remember who said it, but celebrations should only be for people who have something to celebrate."

I lifted the empty glass from Mr. Winters's table, ice still sitting in the bottom, and swept up the damp napkin that had sat beneath it.

"Would you like another one?" I asked, clinking the melting cubes as I gestured with the cup. "I've got plenty of vermouth."

"No, not tonight, Raul, but thank you." Mr. Winters's eyes had not shifted.

I hesitated. It's hard to be young, and I didn't know what to say to this man whom I'd come to think I admired.

I returned to my side of the bar and scooped popcorn from the lit-up popper into a paper boat with red hash lines criss-crossing it.

"Just in case," I said, returning to Mr. Winters's table and placing the corn in the middle of the wood expanse, with a stack of napkins beside it.

On the other side of the glass, three women sang "Pour Some Sugar on Me," arms entwined. Behind me, I felt someone walk into the bar from the clubhouse lounge.

"Good evening, Raul, how goes the fight today?" Mr. Charles's voice carried over the muted singing sneaking in from outside.

"Something like Thermopylae, but I'm hanging in there," I replied, poaching a phrase I'd heard Mr. Winters use. Mr. Winters turned his eyes up to mine for the briefest moment. His lips turned up as well and just as briefly.

Mr. Charles dropped down beside his colleague, and I went to prepare the gimlet I knew the second attorney would want. Behind my bar, I squeezed limes into a cocktail glass. In front of me, the two lawyers sat gazing into the night. On the deck, rich people got drunker and sang flat paeans to their youth.

"Raul, could we get a pitcher of Goose Island and two chardonnays out here?" Mrs. Hanes had recovered herself and poked her head in one of the doors. She smiled and waggled her fingers at me.

"Sure thing, Mrs. H. I'll just get Mr. Charles his gimlet and I'll be right out there."

I hustled around the bar with the pretty beryl drink, set it before Mr. Charles, and returned to my post to fill a plastic pitcher with India pale ale. I'd learned the hard way about serving in glass pitchers at these events. On the deck arranging wine glasses, fresh beer glasses, and the pitcher at Mrs. Hanes's table, I received more drink orders and two orders for onion rings. The work set me moving and I didn't think about the lawyers in the bar or the thickness of their voices when they'd had their heads together. The night had the quality of most June nights on Galveston Bay: soft heat and damp faith and no consciousness of time. I worked the way the club paid me to work, even dancing with Mrs. Hanes to "La Bamba." Such duties had shed their awkwardness and burrs long ago, and she shoved a twenty-dollar bill in my apron at the end of the song. Mr. Winters again sat alone in the bar, and I dumped a tub of dirty glasses in the back and returned to see the older man walking out one of the glass doors onto the deck. I followed that way a moment later with two plates of onion rings, and caught the attorney's white curls disappearing down the outer stairway to the lawn. More glasses gathered, more drinks refilled, and I saw at the base of the lawn, on the old wooden dock the kids used to launch their mini, kid-sized sailboats, Mr. Winters's imposing frame, head bowed.

Even with "Brown Eyed Girl" raining from an amplifier behind me, I heard the splash and then the protest of one of the large water birds that soil the docks.

"Wait," I shouted. "Hey! Mr. Winters fell off the dock."

I knew I was lying. Mr. Winters didn't fall off the dock. Mr. Winters jumped off the dock.

"Hey, someone call 911," I yelled. "Mr. Charles, call 911." I pointed to the lawyer, who'd just stepped onto the deck from the barroom. He looked confused and then pulled his cell phone from a pocket, and I sprinted down the stairs and across the lawn to the dock.

Slabs of moonlight bobbed on the almost-still water and I stood in the dark doing nothing, unsure of everything. People up the lawn called out, and the fuzz that had wrapped around my brain dissolved. I pulled my shoes off and jumped into the harbor. After my own splash, the world turned into simple, wet, dark solitude, and I believed for an instant that I knew why Mr. Winters had come here. Under the water, the world was quiet. It had been so noisy at the club. But down here, everything was easy, whole, still. And then I surfaced. People called out: "Raul! Frank!"

"I'm okay," I shouted. "I'm looking for him." I dove back under the water, back into the noiselessness.

Most of the club's docks floated on plastic pontoons, so the wooden docks could adjust to the rise and fall of water levels, especially storm surges. Members' cats would sometimes tumble off boats and swim up to the docks, and, unable to jump out of the water onto a dock, the animals would instead clamber onto the lower pontoons beneath the docks, sitting in the space between the plastic floats and the wooden planks and meowing their heads off until rescuers arrived with screwdrivers to lift the wooden planks from above and pull the cats up to safety.

I knew where Mr. Winters was. I surfaced for air, took a deep breath, and dove again, swimming under the dock and coming up in the pocket of air beneath it, with the plastic pontoon floats all around me. The attorney bobbed there, his hands pushing against the wooden "roof" of the dock to keep his head from getting bounced into it with the roll of the harbor, the water breathing in and out more slowly than I was.

"Mr. Winters!"

"Hi, Raul."

"Are you okay?" It was hard to see the man in the blackness of the secret space.

"No, Raul."

"Are you hurt? Mr. Charles called 911." Water trickled down my temples, ran from my eyelashes. I tasted salt and felt my undershirt ballooning out under my work shirt, grazing my skin as it swayed with the inlet's roll.

"Not from jumping in the water, son. That actually felt kinda good."

I think the old man was smiling.

"There's just been so much noise," he said. "So many distractions. For far too long. Somewhere along the way, I think I got mixed up." I could feel he was shaking his head in the shadows.

We bobbed there together, listening to the footsteps and shouts and murmurs overhead. I'm not sure if any of the members who had run down to the dock behind me and who now milled on the planks over us could hear us in the water in the almost-coal-mine-dark space beneath their feet.

"What happened? To make you want to go swimming tonight?" I tried to grin. My teeth had started to chatter, the jerking probably more from the release of stress hormones than true cold.

Mr. Winters's chin tilted up and in the blackness it seemed like he was studying the wood of the underside of the dock. Splinters on the planks prickled under my fingers and I hoped none of them would catch in my skin.

"Raul, a jury convicted my client today." Mr. Winters sighed. "It took them thirty-two minutes."

Someone overhead shouted that a police car was pulling into the club.

"They convicted a man of murder," he continued.

I pushed myself along the boards to get closer to him, as people above shifted and a few ran, the footsteps making it hard to hear.

"It was in federal court: murder in Indian Country. A father accused of killing his infant daughter after," he stopped, snorted water from his nose, "after sexually abusing her. It's, it's one of those cases I've told you about, a court-appointed case the federal public defender couldn't take. I don't think the fellow did it, and I think tonight an innocent man is sitting in a cell facing a mandatory life sentence because I couldn't get a jury to look past all the emotion."

The water smacked the bulkhead where the dock attached to the lawn. It bounced off and smacked again. And again.

"It's a long story," Mr. Winters said, "but suffice it to say there just wasn't any real evidence, or at least nothing I could have convicted a man on. Just conjecture." I heard him breathing, like a man who's run a long way in the heat. "And those god-damned pictures of the baby." He sounded strangled, his voice crawling out of a tight space. "She was a beautiful baby." The water was smacking the bulkhead again. "In one of the pictures, she had a pink outfit on just like Meredith had when she was a baby." I'd only met Mr. Winters's oldest daughter, from his first marriage, twice. She lived in California and, as I understood it, seldom made it out to Texas.

I waited. He didn't volunteer anything else. The sound of the water hadn't changed.

"Is it hard?" I asked. "Defending a case like that?"

"It's hard to do anything earnestly," he replied. "It's hard to know you're someone's only chance."

A choked siren sound carried down to us, and I figured Mr. Winters would be in an ambulance in less than three minutes.

"Sounds like the EMTs are here," I whispered.

"I don't need an ambulance, Raul. I don't need anything except a warm blanket and another Negroni. I'm sorry I did this. And I'm really sorry I put a damper on your night."

I heard him chuckle.

"Mr. Winters, it's okay."

"No, the world hasn't been okay in a long, long time, kid. Maybe ever." He snorted again. "It wasn't supposed to be like this."

More shouting overhead and I knew the paramedics were running across the lawn. Tiny sprays of red stars fell through the seams between the dock's wooden planks as emergency lights must have been rotating across the club's parking lot and lawn.

"Here, I'll help you swim out," I whispered, "but, Mr. Winters?" I couldn't tell you where that pause or the following question came from. "Really quickly: what was it supposed to be like?"

In the red-flecked darkness, the old man's eyes looked like fragments cracked off the larger rafts of moonlight floating on the water beyond the cover of the dock. Our cavern smelled of salty oldness, of things unaired.

"Justice, kid, it was supposed to be about justice. With a capital J."

I waited. He inhaled and coughed.

"Kid, it was supposed to be the old 'give me liberty or give me death,' a country founded on man's reason, a bill of rights, constitutional guarantees, the reason all those boys died at Bunker Hill and Shiloh and Normandy. My dad's brother was one of them . . . at Normandy."

Another cough, except we both knew it wasn't really a cough.

"It was supposed to be a jury of one's peers and 'I have a dream' and a nation of laws and not of men. Facing up to crap like My Lai and owning our fuck ups and doing the right thing. It was supposed to be Gideon and a country that loved justice so much it would pay for the defense to oppose its own prosecutorial power. Justice tempered by mercy. It was those women at the Chicago World's Fair who didn't even have the right to vote yet but who fought for public justice."

"Raul? Frank? Are you there?" I thought it was Mr. Charles shouting. I hadn't paid much attention to the members' shouts once I'd gotten under the dock and I felt a bite of guilt for leaving them in their own category of darkness on the lawn.

Maybe Mr. Winters was smiling. "I'm getting old, kid. Here, let's go." He pushed himself toward the pontoons we would have to dive under to return to the "right" side of the dock.

"But wait." He took a hand off the underside of the dock and put it on my shoulder. The water carried him into the wooden planks and the back of his head, neck, and shoulder blades bumped against them. "I failed, Raul. Not the system. The jury did what it thought best. They didn't fail, Raul. I failed."

He pushed off the planks and dove under the surface.

I heard everyone crying out and shouting when he surfaced and then the bumping and pounding of people ostensibly pulling him onto the dock. Tucked away under the din, I felt reluctant to leave my pocket of stillness.

UFO

She scourged the neighborhood, lying in wait atop walls, atop trees, diving upon unsuspecting foe, claws unsheathed. We didn't know if anyone owned her, had never been close enough to check for tags. I fell victim once, one afternoon: victim to the Unidentified Feline Object.

So, yeah, that's how I got this scar.

Feeding Bambi

Two things lay at the root of it all: Daniel had sailed over here from England (like he was British and actually knew the secret of Christmas pudding) and Natalie left. So those factors take care of the causes. As to temporal context, it started around Thanksgiving. A bunch of us went to a beer festival on Galveston Island. Someone had won tickets to the event, tickets that included free beer and food, so of course, we would go. In the throes of an unspeakable struggle with a mediocre chardonnay (and none of us could quite explain the presence of a mediocre chardonnay at a Texas beer festival), Daniel waxed nostalgic for pudding. Real Christmas pudding.

The beer and chardonnay made his tales of ten-pound breads bearing dried fruit and six-penny pieces hidden for the kids—all soaked in brandy, even flaming brandy—especially seductive. After forty-some ounces of lone-star ales and IPAs, and the two ounces of flaccid chardonnay, he declared his intention of initiating us into the rites of the true Christmas pudding. I would finally be a girl who understood the homage to "figgy pudding."

"It sounds disgusting," Natalie said. "Who wants to eat a month-old fruitcake?"

"You've no idea," Daniel replied. "It's gonna be a blinder. Just you wait."

For weeks, we had sensed the impending abandonment. She and Daniel had lived on *Ebb Tide* for six years. Daniel kept the thirty-six-foot cutter in good enough shape (he said shipshape and Bristol fashion, but opinions can differ) and constantly declared they'd push off the dock, bound for the islands across the Gulf, "in just a couple weeks." Meanwhile, Natalie earned ten bucks an hour at a marine-supply store and made her own declarations, namely that she only heard the word "ring" in the context of phones and pugilism.

And then there was the issue of Greg, a rangy Sooner who had arrived at the marina in July with a forty-three-foot Mason, a savings account, and an actual departure date for his trip over the horizon. We'd all seen Greg at the marine store, assiduously measuring out line from the great red-and-white spools of Sta-Set polyester yacht braid, and earnestly inquiring of Natalie her thoughts on composting heads and deep-cycle batteries. Natalie, for her part, seemed amenable enough to stopping by the old Mason and showing Greg how best to tape off teak to prepare it for sanding and refinishing (having had more than a passing amount of practice on *Ebb Tide*).

At the beer fest in Galveston, betrayal lay just on the other side of a couple sunrises. Daniel, however, remained oblivious, whirling instead in his *sui generis* . . . could one say *dhikr?* . . . of detailed descriptions of ten-pound cakes. He went on about daily "feedings" for said cakes, with eighteen-year-old brandy poured over these puddings each day for a month, right up until Christmas when they would be set ablaze before orgiastic consumption on Christmas morning.

"It's settled. I'll dig out my old grandma's recipe, and I shall make us a pudding," he declared. "With currants, raisins, and cranberries, and . . . orange peel. With things you skeptics have never heard of." He laughed as only a salty Brit can laugh.

"But it's not a simple task," he said. "You'll all have to help. We'll do it together. You'll need to remind me to feed it with brandy every day. At my age, I'm liable to forget, you know. So come by the boat every afternoon about teatime and knock on the old girl, and we'll feed the thing together, right?"

I agreed and the others agreed, but Natalie would not agree. She rolled her eyes and turned away and walked off to find some hard cider to sample.

Daniel made very good margaritas, with Espolòn and Cointreau and fresh limes he got at Target about every other day. So generally we didn't want to miss teatime or the pudding feed. It just made sense to give the day a break and feed the pudding and have an early sundowner before Natalie came home and asked Daniel to do something (so then we'd either have to help him with the chore, or go back to our own boats and watch TV, or read of foreign ports we'd get to "one day," or walk the dog, or, best yet, see if anyone had any extra money to do something like go to Galveston for drinks).

After about four or five days of this pudding feeding, someone named the thing Bambi, even though I said it sounded too much like a stripper name, and Bambi stuck, and soon enough, we all talked about heading over to *Ebb Tide* to feed Bambi in the afternoons. Greg, the Sooner with the Mason and the eyes for Natalie, never fed Bambi. He had the dignity to keep his distance from *Ebb Tide* and Daniel.

When I went over, I'd pour brandy over Bambi and into the tin in which she sat. I admired the cake's sugar-glazed skin and deep, nearly scarlet complexion. She had fetching little freckles of dried fruit and nuts poking through, and a luscious aroma that conjured scenes of inebriation and the subsequent swallows of Excedrin.

Natalie had a cat named Angela, who would walk the dock under the pretense that she represented the heavenly host on the Gulf Coast: a great sixteen-pound beast of luscious white locks and *sforzando* purrs. Angela would sit in my lap after the cake feeding and flex her paws and knead the air the way great large cats who think they are angels do.

"What happens if we don't feed it brandy?" I asked Daniel one day, sitting on the settee in the cabin with the cat over my knees.

"Unthinkable," he replied. "The pudding would be ruined. There'd be no hope for it. We have to feed it regularly. A regular intravenous drip . . . with brandy. Get it to the right density and moisture."

When not pulled out for her feeding, Bambi lived under her hood of muslin (tied around the tin with string), steeping in her bath of booze. Natalie never checked on her, much less fed her. Natalie left that to Daniel and me and Daniel's other trusted mates. One evening, Natalie came back to the boat from the marine store and found several of us gathered in *Ebb Tide*'s cockpit, Daniel's margaritas in hand and Bambi tucked away in her place in the galley.

"Glad to see you've all been productive this afternoon," she said, as she stepped aboard and shinnied down the ladder into the cabin.

"Hello to you, too," I yelled after her. Something about Natalie just inclined me toward the unladylike.

Angela leapt off my thighs and followed her mistress below.

"I think I'll pop round to Spec's for more brandy," Daniel said and ducked under the canvas awning that kept the sun out of the cockpit.

The following day when I returned to *Ebb Tide* to feed Bambi, Daniel had Turkish music blaring from the marinized Bose speakers he'd installed in the cockpit the year before, purchasing them with money he'd made at a refinery in Texas City. Natalie wasn't around, nor was Daniel himself, so I unwrapped Bambi's muslin, ladled brandy, and watched the distilled wine seep into flour and ground nutmeg and dried fruit, and ostensibly wash around sixty cents' worth of dimes Daniel had buried in the cake for us "kids" to find, since he hadn't any six-pence pieces to nestle in the dough.

"You want something to drink?" Daniel suddenly appeared in the galley from wherever he'd gotten to while I'd poured hooch over the pudding.

"Sure."

He stepped into the saloon and rummaged in his special cubby he'd lit with blue rope lighting, pulling out a bottle of something clear. In the cockpit, the sun made the water look like lapis and amber run together, and Daniel put on more Turkish music: *rompi rompi* and then Tarkan. He handed me a tin mug with something smelling of anise. The last time Daniel made money was on a short hop to Turkey for something oil related.

"I need to fix this," he said, stomping a little on the cockpit floor.

I shuffled my flip flops off and bounced on the sole, too.

"Yeah, it's soft," I agreed.

"Rotten," he said. "See there? That crack in the fiberglass? Water's gotten in and rotted the core."

"It'll be a pain in the ass," I said.

"No choice," he said. "I'll have to cut this piece out, glass in a new core. Then glass the whole thing back into place."

"That'll take a lot of work," I said.

"Nothing else to be done. I can't go cruising with the cockpit the way it is."

I sat down again. I didn't like licorice, but I drank the thing Daniel had mixed up anyway, considered it *exotic*.

"If I'm gonna get this job done, I'd better get some tools from storage," Daniel said. "You can stay here. I've gotta get some marine-grade plywood, too. I don't have any. Job'll cost me a monkey at least."

He dropped into the cabin again, and I heard him rattle keys around.

"You stay here. Keep an eye on Bambi," he said a minute later when he emerged and then stepped over onto the dock. "Feed 'er a little more when you finish that drink, if you like. I'll be back in a bit." He turned, gave a half-smile. "No pinching any."

He left, and I finished the drink and poured a little more brandy over the cake, and then I took off to find something to do. The following day, someone else must have fed Bambi because I got a gig cleaning a big Hatteras sport-fishing boat and didn't see Daniel. When next I saw him, Daniel had *Ebb Tide*'s cockpit sole cut out, a gaping wound open in her deck where the rotted flooring had been. He had 5200 sealant and sheets of fiberglass and bottles of epoxy resin and hardener arrayed over the benches of the cockpit. On the cabin top, beside the companionway, a quart of acetone perched next to a tray of wooden sticks and brushes and rags.

"Bambi's looking right perky down there," he called out from where he stood on *Ebb Tide*'s bowels, beneath where the floor of the cockpit should have been.

"Only two more days," I said. It was December 23rd and we had big plans for a Christmas breakfast at the pavilion. Lucas from dock eighteen would bring his guitar up, and the old couple who lived on the homemade catamaran were preparing a turkey, and I had two cans of creamed corn and a box of Jiffy cornbread mix to turn into my never-famous corn casserole, if I remembered to fill my propane tank, so I could light the oven. No one had invited Greg the Sooner.

"Is Natalie excited to try the pudding now?" I had a terrible habit of attempting to be upbeat and falling flat on banal.

"No, she's a bit of a damp squib over the whole thing, but never mind. Bambi's going to be a real belter."

"Well, I'm excited about it." I minced around the chasm, guiltily enjoying the fumes of boat work, and dropped in to check on Bambi and run her bath for her.

"You need a hand with anything?" I asked Daniel after I'd attended to the cake.

"No, thanks. It's all sorted." He gestured at the plywood core he'd swaddled in fiberglass and slathered with epoxy.

On Christmas Eve, I waited till a little past six to amble over to *Ebb Tide*, hoping for a dinner invitation from Daniel and Natalie because no one wants to eat Christmas Eve dinner alone, and I carried with me a glass baking dish, the Jiffy mix, the cans of corn, a tub of sour cream, two sticks of butter, and a wilted bag of cheddar cheese (the cheese all clinging kinda sadly to the see-through plastic of the bag in the still-warm Texas sun). I hadn't gotten the propane, and I hoped I could use *Ebb Tide*'s little Force Ten oven to mix my magic.

Nothing in the cockpit had changed other than Murat Boz had usurped Tarkan's place of prominence and now sprayed modern Anatolia over the marine construction supplies and Daniel's hunched back. A rag sat stuffed in the top of the acetone bottle, which had moved down to the space under the cockpit beside Daniel, who was fiddling with sandpaper and his unwieldly piece of fiberglass-wrapped plywood.

"Can I use your oven to make my corn thing?" I asked Daniel, finding it difficult to hop aboard a boat with no clear flooring when my hands were full of casserole fixings.

"Help yourself. Make yourself at home," he mumbled from the crevasse. "Natalie's gone and told me to get fucked, so the place is all yours."

"What happened?" I knew (anyone would have known), but I asked anyway out of a dumb lack of originality.

"Tell you later," Daniel said. "Don't want to talk about it."

"Okay."

In the galley, I *mise-en-placed* and preheated the oven.

Daniel appeared in the companionway, a great misplaced, backlit Drake or Nelson or Cook, daubed in epoxy and 5200 and splotches of thinner.

"Bitch just up and left this afternoon." He didn't wash his hands or put a towel out to protect the settee before he flopped down on it. "I'm sure she's over on that Mason with that bastard Okie." He said Okie the way I might say wanker.

"I'm sorry, Daniel." I didn't turn away from Bambi because the whole thing made my skin crawl.

"It's a load of bollocks." He scooted over to the blue-lit cubby.

Then "Miserlou"—a real Greek rendition, not the Dick Dale one—rolled over us, and Daniel held up a bottle of ouzo.

"Sure," I said.

Ouzo and Lebanon's Nancy Ajram will make a lot of things hurt less, and we weren't hurting much at all when Natalie banged on *Ebb Tide*'s hull around midnight. By then, Lucas and Tyler and Diane had come over, and we had started trying to sing along to Nancy's Arabic lyrics.

"Who's down there? Are you drunk down there?" Natalie yelled louder than she needed to.

"No." Daniel yelled even louder.

"I want to get Angela."

I realized Natalie's cat was still in the boat. I hadn't thought about it. The great white thing sat in Diane's lap and Diane had a brush full of cat hair in her hand.

"Come get your damn cat then," Daniel shouted.

Natalie backed down the ladder into the cabin. She didn't say anything. She took hold of the oversized feline and stumbled trying to climb the ladder and get off the eviscerated boat, the cat squirming and yowling. (That was the last I saw of her, though I know she moved onto that Mason. I avoided the Mason's dock after that night.)

"Fuck her," Diane said after the silence had washed out through the companionway behind Natalie, and the sticky, false conviviality had returned.

Lucas passed around a bottle of schnapps he'd brought with him.

"Where's the cake? Where's Bambi?" he asked.

"Ah, beloved, constant, felicitous Bambi," Daniel cooed. "Oh, good ol' Bambi."

No one rose, but we all turned toward the galley. The swaddled bowl sat in a nook beside the sink.

"Well, what are we waiting for? Jolly old Saint Nick himself? It's Christmas. Let's eat the pudding." Daniel jumped up, making *Ebb Tide* rock a little. "Let's eat the goddamned pudding." Then he fixed his eyes on us. "Y'all," he tried to drawl.

He brushed past our knees as he passed through the saloon toward the galley. We watched as he ceremoniously peeled back Bambi's veil.

"Oh, what a beautiful, brilliant thing you are." He threw open a cupboard and his icebox, pulling out and halving a lime and dropping sugar cubes into a cup of brandy.

"What'd I tell ya? It's a blinder. It's all right. This will be right. This one thing will be right and good and perfect!" He had started shouting. "Come on! Let's eat under the stars."

I looked at Tyler and Diane and Lucas, and they looked back at me, and for a minute, I didn't feel so drunk . . . just uncomfortable.

"Come on!" Daniel shouted again. "Someone grab that bottle of brandy." He cocked his head toward the saffron bottle beside the sink.

Then he clasped Bambi to himself and grasped the cup holding the brandy-glutted sugar cubes and half a lime, and then sprang up the ladder.

We rose, and I think I was not alone in feeling some reluctance to join our friend beneath the yuletide stars shining over the cockpit awning. But we shuffled up after him. Lucas picked up the bottle of brandy, and Diane asked if something was burning as she passed the galley, mumbling about whether it looked like smoke was coming from the oven and didn't it smell like smoke. No one looked back or answered her. We marched up the ladder and found our leader balanced in the hole where the cockpit floor had been, the acetone bottle balanced at his feet, the epoxies arrayed around him.

Daniel crowned Bambi Queen of the World and placed the half lime on her bosom. Circling the lime, he arranged the brandy-soaked sugar cubes.

"Now isn't that nearly perfect?" He looked up at us in the starlight and we looked back and the awning made everything very dark.

From somewhere, Daniel produced a sprig of plastic holly and set it atop our sugary regent. Over it all, he dribbled the last of the brandy from the bottle Lucas handed him.

"Now give me a lighter," he cried. "Merry Christmas, all! Merry Christmas!"

We looked at him in the booze- and fumes-soaked air.

Then he tilted his head back and screamed: "Merry Crimbo!"

Daniel's shibboleth was the last clear thing. Lucas dug a Bic out of his jeans and handed it to Daniel. And that action set the metal wheel of fate grinding. Daniel sparked the Bic, and for all the watery world to see, Bambi blazed like the Star of Bethlehem, and then the Bic burned Daniel's fingers, and Bambi dropped to his feet, and the acetone turned a bit of debris into a Molotov cocktail, and the propane line feeding the oven (which had indeed been on—burning my corn) burst, and the once gutted cockpit turned Roman candle, and *Ebb Tide*'s stern shot into the heavens, and we shot into the night, and the water was very cold when I landed, and Daniel splashed somewhere nearby, and I hate to think what that no-good Okie said about it all when he heard the story from the dock gossips in the morning.

A real blinder. . . .

Communion

Beneath unruly silver hair, an elderly man in the pew in front of mine sorts through a stack of junk mail as I wait for the usher to invite me to enter the Communion line.

A Jetty

"Every couple needs a *thing*."

She'd laughed as she'd said it, holding her phone out, insisting she could get the roller coaster, its red and orange lights on the boardwalk behind them, into the frame with them. That was on their fourth date. He remembered it. He remembered the sand in her hair, and he remembered the salt-taste of her lips and the seagulls screaming over the trash bins on the seawall.

So even all these years later, after everything that didn't work, after everything that didn't make her get better, that didn't fix it or stop what happened, or make the ending something else, he still ends up on this jetty, on this day, at this time. Looking out to the horizon and watching the freighters. It's easy to fit everything into the photo's frame now. Except, of course, it isn't.

A Chain of Texts

The first text arrived at 10:52 a.m.

> Parents, we must alert you that Lakeview High School has experienced an emergency and is in lock-down status. State authorities are on their way. We cannot release further details at this time, but we will alert you once the situation is contained. Please do not call for information, as staff are not available to respond at this time.

With everything in the news, of course, my mind leaped to the worst possible scenario: a school shooting. Brett and I had had an altercation with Chloe the night before and she hadn't spoken to us that morning as we'd ground coffee and fried eggs. She'd left without eating anything, and I regretted what I'd said about her weight the night before. I only wanted her to be healthy.

My mouth was dry as I looked at the screen, the gray bubble of message. I texted Chloe. I'd seen those texts online from parents and kids when that shooter went on a rampage at the Florida school. What if?

> Honey, are you OK? Honey, I'm sorry about last night. Your dad and I love you so much. You can't imagine how much you mean to us. We love you more than anything. I know it's been hard lately, but everything's going to be better. Please let me know you're all right. 😢💜💜💜😢

The school's second text arrived at 11:01 a.m.

> Parents, we must inform you that we have verified the disturbance at Lakeview High School. A student opened fire in a classroom this morning. Authorities have arrived, but the situation remains critical. Media outlets have arrived and we want to make sure we provide you with accurate information as soon as possible. We are, however, in a state of emergency, as the shooter has taken

> four students and a teacher hostage. We regret we cannot provide further information at this time. We are doing everything in our power to contain the situation.

Because three coworkers rushed into my office panicked, I knew I had screamed. I dropped my phone and the screen cracked, and the crack spread all over, so it was hard to see to text Chloe again, but I had to get to her because I *knew*, I just knew, she was in that classroom with some crazed, psychopathic killer holding a gun to her head, screaming at her—at my Chloe—at the baby girl I'd prayed to God to give me, whom I'd nursed and sung to and bought a stuffed monkey for—we'd called Chloe Monkey after that for like two years, and she'd always giggled when we'd asked if the Monkey wanted a banana.

> Chloe, sweetheart, you're everything to us. You're the only thing. I can't imagine a world without you. You're our happiness and I love and everything we we've ever wanted and more. I love you. I love you.

When I saw the text an instant after tapping to send it, I saw those stupid locks. I'd wanted the heart—the heart, goddamnit.

♥ ♥ ♥

There.

I'd fixed it. I could fix this. God would fix this. I'd see her again. I'd see my Chloe. I'd get her back. Why did we scream like that sometimes, she and I? Why had I ever said anything vicious to her? To my baby.

> Chloe, sweetheart, I love you I love you I lone too pledge sweetheart please tell me your ok pledge let me know your ok dad and I live you I live you Your mom loves you so much baby

An alert appeared on my phone's screen at 11:16 a.m.

> News Top Stories
> At least 5 killed in shooting at Lakeview High School in Houston, Texas; the suspect believed to be a student and is currently holding three students hostage—VM News

Wait, three students held hostage? No, it was four. And a teacher. They'd missed two people. They'd missed Chloe. That shooter hadn't shot Chloe, hadn't killed her. Couldn't have. Not my Chloe. No, they were wrong. Those people weren't dead. It was five hostages, not three.

The school's third text arrived at 11:28 a.m.

> Parents, authorities have taken the shooter into custody. Two of the hostages have survived and are being taken to the medical center now. Ambulances and medical personnel are on site to respond to the situation. The police are working to restore order. We cannot respond to phone or electronic communications at this time, but police have established a perimeter around the school and we ask you to follow their orders as you come to pick up your students.

Pick up Chloe? I could pick up Chloe. Chloe was at the school. She was at the school. She was okay. She was alive. She was okay.

"Brett," I screamed.

I was screaming into the phone. I don't know why I hadn't called him before, why I couldn't feel my legs, why Rachel's arms felt weird and sticky around me, why the area around my desk smelled like the garage on hot days when the garbage can got really full.

"Brett, she's okay. She must be okay. She's alive. Brett, she's alive. She has to be okay."

I couldn't hear him answering me. I couldn't hear anything. The blood in my ears was too loud, my body was too loud, the office was too loud, the whole goddamned fucking world was too loud.

The last text came at 11:52 a.m. The phone screen was still all spider-web cracked and the words beneath the cracks were splintered, and I fainted after that, and Rachel must have called 911.

> Mrs. Davis, I'm Officer Maxine Walker with the Houston Police Department. We have taken your daughter Chloe Davis into custody in connection with the shooting at Lakeview High School this morning. You can contact me at this number for further details.

On Staying

Neither of my parents stayed with me past my teenage years—my mother not at all and my father lingered only in odd, infrequent phone calls and unveiled inquiries after money.

I, for my part, didn't stay either . . . failed to stay with any of the husbands I'd sworn (literally on a Bible) to stay beside till death did us part. Death, I suppose, did part us, but of course it wasn't *that* kind of death, a bodily death of either of us—it was death of something that doesn't count when you've sworn on a Bible.

Even Jesus didn't stay. After the priest scandals (one after another, even long after they were supposed to have passed), after the apologies read from ambos facing empty pews, the recorded voices of saddened bishops spilling from stereos plugged in before vigil masses, Jesus was gone. Because, of course, he'd left his church. How else could a church end up like that? And probably his mother hadn't stayed either. In the church, I mean.

Except one

day I saw an old couple in a coffee shop. He was sitting in a wheelchair (and not a nice one, not one that looked like someone had bought it with insurance funds, not one with electrical mechanisms to perhaps make something like being in it easier). She wore a shirt obviously from somewhere like Walmart, and most likely from Walmart by way of somewhere like Goodwill. He was lifting a jacket from his lap in that wheelchair, and she got up from her seat at that small round table (obviously with aching knees and lower back and the delay age imposes on things like that, like getting up from a table). And she reached over and took that jacket and draped that jacket around his shoulders. And then she sat back down, and they both sipped coffee. Neither of them said anything, or didn't say anything out loud. Because she *did* leave an arm around him—he hunched forward in that chair.

And then she rose again (again with the obvious cracks and cavitations) and turned to push him toward the coffee-shop door, and I suddenly wanted to be some ancient mendicant, wanted to reach out to touch some garment's hem, that jacket's hem, that worn-out, wrong-color Walmart shirt's hem, to receive some (please pardon a most horrible pun—if it is a pun, and not just a terrible choice of words—pardon it either way, if you will) staying power.

Because it seemed that these two *had* stayed. That *something* had stayed.

But (of course) I did not reach out. How could I? Why would I? I did smile, though. And when the woman met my eyes, she smiled, and I think her smile stayed for a long time afterward.

*

The rain-pocked card beside the headstone read
Happy Anniversary.

Closed

I knew when I married Kurt that I was marrying the boys, too. The situation worried me: I've never wanted kids. I've never looked at a baby and thought, "I want that." When I first met the boys—first met Brenner and Quinn—it was rocky. Kurt took all of us to Maggiano's and we ate too much pasta and tiramisu and I asked the boys about school and whether Quinn was nervous about starting high school in the fall. He's the oldest, the trailblazer. Neither kid said much, leaving me and their dad with those one-word answers my kid-possessing colleagues at the public-defender's office complain about in the breakroom every lunch hour.

So when I discovered the La Porte community wave pool after the wedding and moving in with Kurt, I felt like I had a chance. Kurt and I discussed it first and he gave me the green light to text the boys, who spend most nights at their mom's place, and invite them for an afternoon of tubing in man-made waves. It took a couple hours, but each boy texted back "sure" to my pitiful, plaintive "would you guys like to go to the wave pool in La Porte next week?"

I scheduled a "personal day" and packed up a canvas tote bag with boardshorts and a long-sleeved rashguard (I fear the sun and public exposure of a body that no longer showcases bathing suits well), a bikini no one would ever see (thanks to those outer layers), towel, sunscreen (the spray-on kind that kids are supposed to prefer), and the sundry items required for a trip to water in the summer.

And then I waited. In my head, I debated about how to handle lunch with the kids. Buy sandwiches at the pool? Take them someplace nicer afterward? Would that mean eating too late? Would I be expected to police nutrition—like should I let them order soda? Ice cream? Such anxieties led to larger preoccupations. Would it be okay to let them run around the complex alone or should I stay with them at all times? Would Quinn feel embarrassed being there with me (he's fourteen now)? (I figured Brenner, who's ten, still went everywhere with his mom, so I'd just be a proxy for that supervision. But was that assumption true? Would he resent me intruding on an adventure he believed he should have been sharing with his mother?)

"Do you want to take the day off and come with us," I asked Kurt two nights before the outing. "No, not at all," he replied. "I think this will be great for you and the boys. I'm looking forward to hearing how it goes," he said. I fell asleep and had a dream about floating alone in the middle of the ocean. It was very, very hot in the dream and the sun beat down on me and I was extremely thirsty. When the dream faded, I woke up (about two a.m.), and I really was thirsty, so I went in the bathroom and got a cup of water, and I thought about how Kurt had laughed when Quinn asked, at dinner a few nights before the wedding, if we really did have to get married because his dad getting married again was such a bummer.

When I pulled into the boys' mom's driveway the morning of Operation Wave Pool, I checked my purse a third time to make sure I had enough cash for the entry fees and lunch and for unforeseen expenses. I had $150. That would be fine, I told myself. It took almost ten minutes for the boys to come out of the house, and neither one smiled when I said "good morning." They put their bags in the back of the car and didn't say anything when they got into the backseat. As I drove, I heard them snickering, and in the rearview mirror, I saw them staring into their phones.

A German sedan cut me off in traffic, and I honked and mumbled "fuck you." And then I remembered the boys and felt like I'd somehow failed in some small way, and I thought about them telling their mom that Paulette had said "fuck you" to someone. I didn't know if I should apologize or pretend it didn't happen. I was still worrying about it when I pulled up at the wave pool. But then I stopped worrying about it—about that, about the "fuck you"—because I parked . . . and the sign read "closed."

On Leaving

"It's not *doubt*, Michael. Your parents aren't moving away from here because of doubt. It's *drought*." Michael's teacher smiled.

Michael shook his head. Even at six years old, he knew she was wrong. Sure, the adults of the valley were leaving because the plants were dying, but Michael knew all the rest, too.

Corpus Crispy

My dad always said I could use the boat. My stepmom did, too. They met sailing, and after they started dating—when I was about ten years old—they bought this wrecked old 1979 Cal sailboat. She's twenty-nine feet long, the boat is, and when they got her, back when I was a kid, she was twenty-nine feet of beat-to-hell fiberglass, and the ropes were all frayed, and the sun had destroyed the canvas and Dacron sail material.

Now, though, the boat looks pretty nice. My dad's an engineer and my stepmom's a lawyer, and they spend a lot of time and money on the boat. For the longest time, I wasn't interested in it, but now that it's too late, and I'll be leaving for college in less than a year, I want to get to know her—get to know the boat. I've come to like the old girl. This fall, I asked my dad if I could have a key to the gate at the marina and to the lock on the boat's companionway, and he said yes. Every few weekends now, I drive the three and a half hours from Houston to Corpus Christi to see her.

When I make this trip, I pack a waterproof duffle with shorts, a hoodie, a book, and a notebook I've been making notes in for the last couple of years. It's not worth calling it a journal, but it's something like that. I tell my dad before I go, so he and my stepmom won't go down there and run into me.

When this evening started, I wasn't thinking about going down to the old boat (her name is *Catharsis*). But after the football game (we won; I rushed for over a hundred yards) and after the dance started and after Serefina's friend Bridget finally left us alone, I started thinking about *Catharsis*.

Now, "Despacito" is playing, and I don't need to hear "Despacito" again. Serefina is pressed up against me—which isn't bad—and the AP English teacher's eyes have glazed over, so she looks like a scarecrow planted in the corner of the multipurpose room.

"You ready to go?" I ask Serefina.

She opens her eyes and tilts her head up to look at me. She's pretty short. She says petite. We aren't like that (like keeping the rubber plantations in Cameroon in business) and we don't drink and I've never tried weed, so I think maybe I surprised her with my invitation to blow the dance.

"What do you mean?" she asks.

"Let's go. I got an idea."

"Okay."

We get in the old Samurai my dad bought me for my seventeenth birthday, and I turn the radio on. It has a real radio: like AM, FM, and all that. There is no Bluetooth or anything. I surf through some stations, and I can't say why, but I leave it on Delilah, the old-lady DJ with the sappy show about appreciating life and loved ones. She chooses a song for some lady's husband who is overseas (and will, ostensibly, only hear about this musical selection when his old lady DMs him about it): "Iris" by the Goo Goo Dolls. My mom listens to this station. I make my way to the Beltway and then onto 59 south.

Serefina reaches around the stick and sets her hand on my thigh. We ride that way till the Buc-ee's gas station in Wharton, north of El Campo. With its snapped-on vinyl top and the rush of its own speed, the Samurai is loud and we don't talk much till I pull off at the Buc-ee's to get fuel and snacks. And then it comes to me, beneath the yellow-light grin of the patron beaver of all lone-star roadtrips: the idea of how we'll spend our last homecoming.

"'Fina, how about this, babe? How about we spend the rest of the night sampling the best of the Coastal Bend's fast-food cuisine?"

"What?" She maybe dozed off a little and now sounds kind of groggy.

"We're going to go to all the fast-food restaurants in Corpus Christi and get the best item from each one."

"Why?"

"Because. We'll start here, so it'll be Corpus Christi and beyond. Just one thing from each place. Or maybe one thing for each of us, so really two things. Buc-ee's: I'm gonna say kolaches. Unless you want jerky, babe."

"Ew."

We get out of the Samurai and she waddles next to me in her CFMs, leaning on my arm.

"Those shoes are stupid," I tell her.

"I know."

"I have shower sandals in my bag. You can use them."

"They'll be too big."

"Anything's better than what you got on."

"Okay."

Neither of us considers trying to find a pair of sandals at the Bucee's.

'Fina ducks into the ladies' room and I grab six glass bottles of something by Starbucks. I want to see the dawn with her, so we'll need those. Then, I approach the kolache counter, row upon row of beautiful buns.

"Jalapeño cheese and one pecan pie," I tell the woman. She tongs the rolls into two bags—each bun gets its own sack—and hands them over to me.

'Fina limps up behind me and puts a hand on my shoulder. She doesn't say anything, just takes one of the bags and peeks in. She smiles.

In the jeep, we debate the rules of the game.

"Do we get to share in this scenario?" Serefina asks.

"I dunno. What do you think?"

"I think we should share. Allows for a greater range of culinary experience." She giggles.

"Okay."

We sit in the Samurai, parked next to the gas pump, and she opens the bag with the jalapeño-cheese one in it. "Let's start here. You can do the honors."

She holds the bun up to me and grins. She's leaning over the stick, her left leg tucked up under her as she twists toward me, the foot wrapped around her right calf. Her stilettos have flopped over on their sides, empty and forsaken in the footwell. She shuts her eyes and kisses my ear and then puts the roll in my mouth. I bite into it.

Then she sits back, leans against the little truck's door, and takes her own bite.

"I like these," she says. "I know I shouldn't. They're like total crap. Sodium and bleached flour and mystery meat. But they taste good."

Her mom is a vegetarian yoga teacher and 'Fina doesn't eat a lot of hot dogs or pepperoni pizza.

When we finish the jalapeño-cheese kolache in a few bites, I start the engine and pull out of the gas station. 'Fina pulls the pecan bun out. We pass through El Campo, Edna, and Victoria. The night is warm. My stepmom's from Michigan and she talks about how much she hates the snow; I can't imagine anything but this warmth, the South's forgiveness. Sure, there's the rain—and the storms—but there's always the warmth, the dirty pink color of sunset spread out over the Gulf, the truth of Galveston Bay and its brown-mud water you can't look down into, can't see through.

At Victoria, I pick up 77 toward Refugio, where I fork down to Copano Bay. One of the Starbucks drinks volunteers for duty when I yawn. We've been watching the trucks hauling other old trucks, everything laden with riding lawn mowers, old bikes, and washing machines bound for points far south, places perhaps like Veracruz, where 'Fina's dad's folks are from, or maybe even farther . . . Guatemala City or one of the towns where 'Fina's mom sometimes teaches yoga retreats for women from the Woodlands who want "an adventure," some town named in a Mayan dialect so it's hard to pronounce. But now I'm alone because 'Fina has dozed off.

We cross the Aransas River, tabular, marshy land pressed flat by the black sky, a worn-out work shirt a star-spangled wife irons for Orion. The bridge is all lit up and the U.S.S. Lexington is the color of some of the girls' dresses from the dance earlier. Serefina sleeps with her head against the window and her bare feet on the rubber floor mat, her knees knocked in against each other. I pull onto Shoreline and pass the first turn to a T-head. At the second turn—to the Lawrence Street T-Head—I shift down to second and spin the wheel to the left. In the city-marina parking lot, I kill the engine and step out and look up.

'Fina stirs. "Where are we?"

"My dad's boat's marina."

"Huh?"

"I'm gonna go to the bathroom real quick and we'll stretch our legs and then we're going to McDonald's for french fries."

"Are you serious?"

"Yeah. Have a coffee." I reach between the seats and grab one of the glass bottles and hand it to her.

She takes it and opens her door. She starts to dink with the CFMs.

"Hang on." I pull the driver seat forward and unzip my gym bag sitting on the tiny rear bench. I don't need to see; I can feel the bumpy plastic of the shower sandals as I grope in the duffle.

"Here." I pull the sloppy shoes out and walk around the back of the truck. I kneel and slide these plastic slippers onto Cinderella's feet. She kisses the top of my head and steps out of the jeep, adjusting her dress and its deep slit.

In the oversized sandals, she shuffles next to me, holding the coffee bottle, as I walk to the bathhouse.

"Better?" I ask.

"Much."

After the bathhouse, we climb back into the Samurai, and I take us down Ocean Drive toward the twenty-four-hour Mac-y D's.

"So what's the best thing at Mickey D's?" I ask her as I pull into the drive-thru. It's hard for me to choose between calling it Mac-y D's and Mickey D's. "I'm saying french fries. What do you think?"

"Milkshake. Chocolate." She's leaning into me, her breasts satin in the dress . . . her hair satin, too, I guess I'd say.

"Shit," I *actually* say, looking at my watch in the fluorescence of the drive-thru window. "Sonic closes at midnight."

I pay for the McDonald's and turn left. Past the Pizza Hut, I turn left again and nose into a stall at the Sonic drive-in.

"Quick, quick, quick, Cinderella, what's it gonna be?"

"Tater tots for you and a Classic Crispy Chicken Sandwich for me."

"Tater tots? When we've got the fries?"

"You said you wanted the best thing at each place. It's tots here. And more shakes. But we already have the Mickey D's shake."

"You always right. Tots it is."

I push the button and a woman responds.

"We missed Arby's," 'Fina says, looking into her phone. "Closes at eleven. Tragic. I like the Bronco-berry sauce on the jalapeño poppers."

"Are you serious? Arby's?"

"Don't hate."

A chick emerges from the building with a tray of tots and the sandwich. I hand her a ten and she gives me change. I give her back a buck.

"Now where?" 'Fina looks at the paper sack of McDonald's fries, the shake, the paper-wrapped chicken sandwich, and the poster-board tray of tots. "We're gonna be sick."

"We're not done."

I take Staples Street back into the city and we park near B dock, which houses *Catharsis*. I carry the four remaining bottles of coffee and the tots, and 'Fina takes the rest. At the gate to the dock, I push a hip pocket toward 'Fina and she reaches into it, finding the magnetic key. She looks at me, and I nod toward the corresponding magnetic panel fixed beside the gate. She swipes the key in front of the panel, and we're in.

"She's up here on the left," I whisper, as we walk past a sport-fishing boat, an old Hunter, and a Mason 43.

"This one," I say when we reach old *Catharsis*.

'Fina waits for me to climb aboard. I balance the tots and coffees and step over the lifelines. I put the paper tray and bottles on top of the companionway and reach back for Serefina's burden. Once her hands are free, I take hold of her and bring her into the cockpit, the shower sandals dangling from her feet as she steps over the stainless lifelines.

"Welcome aboard S/V *Catharsis*," I say, sweeping my arms.

She wrinkles her nose.

Overhead, stars stand and wait for God's next waltz. The city's lights outline Serefina, her dress cleaving to her, the slit very high after the step over the lifelines. I kiss her: tongue and hope, and her acceptance at UT Austin and mine at A and M (and how far away we will be, even though it doesn't look that far on the map), and the two years we've been together, and the taste of coffee. Then I unlock the companionway and slide the hatch back and we take the food below to the wooden table my dad refinished last year. 'Fina sits so her feet rest in my lap as we share milkshake and fried potatoes, and neither of us can bring ourselves to finish the Classic Crispy Chicken Sandwich.

"I just can't," she protests, putting a hand on her soft satin belly. Then she laughs. "A Classic Crispy Chicken Sandwich for a Classic Corpus Crispy night."

I lean over and run a hand up the un-slit leg, the one covered by satin, up over the belly, to a breast that fits in my palm just so. It's one of those things that has always fit perfectly. And I kiss her again, awkward lean and feet in ribs, until she gently kicks her feet free and wraps her legs around me, and there's satin, and night outside a little boat on a soft Gulf bay.

"We're not done," I whisper after tasting the backs of her teeth.

"No, we're not," she says, sitting up.

"Come on." I reach down for the sandals on the cabin sole and slide them onto her feet again. I pull her up. We climb into the cockpit and back onto the dock and I check that I have the key.

On the seawall, a group of people our age sit and shout about the boats, and one calls the other a *pendejo*, and a girl passes a package of cigarettes around. We cross Shoreline Boulevard and turn left, the Whataburger a big orange lighthouse shining over the harbor.

I look at Serefina.

"It's the sauce here that matters," she responds. "The food's not as important as the sauce. Like the Bronco-berry sauce at Arby's."

I slip my hand down off her waist to points south as we stand in front of the register.

"Number fourteen," she says to the dude in front of us. "The Whatachick'n Bites with jalapeño-ranch sauce. And can we get honey barbeque, too?"

"Sure." The dude takes the money I hand across the counter.

Serefina accepts the paper bag when it comes up. "We got the toast, too. That's important. The toast." She pats the stripes of the orange-and-white sack.

We don't return to the docks and *Catharsis* but instead walk toward the Selena Memorial. We don't talk, don't discuss where we are going or what to do. We walk, walk past the Lawrence T-head, walk toward Selena at the white cenotaph, toward the pretty bronze performer leaning against the pillar in her sculpted jacket and tight metal pants. Even at this hour, half a dozen people with cameras listen to the *cumbia* and words of the recorded tribute to the singer, and colored lights spill purple and green over the statue. My mind links the scent of paper-bagged chicken nuggets and will-be-prom-queen perfume with the color purple after midnight, and it bonds the color green to the song of elderly Hispanic women whispering about the beauty of a dead *reina de Tejano* music.

"I like it here," Serefina says beside the memorial, stepping up on the white balustrade atop the seawall and leaning over toward the boats in their berths in the marina across the water. "I really do."

She turns and hikes her dress up and I see a sliver of pink lace, and she climbs on my back, wraps her legs around me, and her arms wrap around my neck, the Whataburger bag dangling in front of my chest. I carry her around the corner of the memorial and down the seawall a few yards and then back. Then she slides off and lands on the plastic sandals and dashes, as best she can in those sandals, down the concrete steps beside the memorial. I follow her. She stops at the bottom of the stairs.

"Here," she says. "Hang on."

She walks toward the edge of the seawall and the water and slips the sandals off and leaves them there, nestling the Whataburger bag on top of them, and then picks her way around black stains of gum to return to the base of the steps. She balances on her toes.

"Remember me like this," she says. She adjusts her dress, taking hold of the satin and fanning it out. Hair falls in her face and she poses against the cement base of the memorial.

"Here wait," she says.

And I do. I remember her like that.

And then she pushes her hair back and looks up and holds her dress out, the slit at just the right place on her thigh, and *cumbia* plays overhead in the shrine and the boats breathe behind me in their berths and Orion's wife keeps ironing the world flat overhead.

*

He's old and smells of something acidic, missing a leg but not a smile as he holds open the station door. She doesn't have any cash for the paper cup he has in his hand, so she uses a different door as she hurries to catch her train.

Milwaukee

Maybe different cities have different kinds of cold. Or maybe places in general have different colds. When the bus stopped in Chicago, the driver opened the door and cold swept in, but it wasn't like the cold we'd left in Michigan, and it wasn't like the cold of a Marshals lockup. The Chicago cold had sharper edges. Cold in Michigan had been worn out, with rounded corners, used up and yielding. And cold in a lockup is its own thing.

The hurt of the Chicago cold made me resent Jacob.

"It's fuckin' freezing, man," I shouted to him over the voices of two women on cell phones calling their people for rides from the bus station.

"It ain't so bad." Years ago, Jacob read a couple self-help books and became a this-ain't-so-bad type of person.

"Do you know where the fuck we're going? Let's find a bus to Milwaukee." I stopped in front of the door to the station, scanning the placards of the buses at the curb.

"I ain't gettin' on no more buses today." Jacob's breath puffed in front of his lips, and we were both shouting a little because of the wind and the general noise of travel, of people going somewhere else.

"Well, I ain't wanderin' around this city in this fuckin' cold, man." I shoved my hands in the pockets of my jacket. It was an old jacket and made for fall, not winter—and we were beyond fall cold.

"We'll play some music. Then maybe we can get a decent dinner." Jacob took a few steps and rounded the corner of the bus station, and I followed him because I didn't want to argue and I wasn't much in the mood for another bus ride either.

The sun felt weak and like it didn't want to crawl past the buildings to the concrete and dirty puddles and gum stains on the sidewalks, and as we walked across the river and past the city's Chipotles and Burger Kings, I shivered. Jacob stopped on a corner next to a big Macy's and said we could set up and play there, and I resented him even more.

"I ain't playin' here. It's fuckin' cold, man. Plus, you probably need a license or something to play on the street. I don't want to deal with that bullshit."

"Shut up already about the cold." He pulled a Martin Backpacker out of his bag. The guitar had been in the trunk when we'd gotten arrested on I-94.

I dug in my backpack for a harmonica. My lips had cracked, and my hands felt too heavy to play. "I can't, man. Let's just go find a bus. This is fuckin' crazy."

"Where you want to go?" Jacob fiddled with the guitar's tuning pegs.

"I don't know. Not here." I hunched my shoulders and turned my back to the wind.

"Houston?" He stopped working on the strings and looked at me.

I stared back at him.

"Corpus?" He strummed the guitar and made another adjustment. "Aw, fuck no. I ain't goin' back there."

He leaned down and pulled a capo out of the bag he'd dropped at his feet. Neither of us spoke again until he launched into "Wagon Wheel" and he started singing to people walking past about his plan to head down south, to the land of the pines, and thumb his way to North Caroline. Toward the end of the song, a kid stopped in front of me. He looked about eight years old.

"Come on, honey." The woman with the kid pulled on the kid's arm.

But the kid kept standing there, watching us. He smiled, and the woman pulled again.

"Honey, come on."

She picked the boy up. He watched me over her shoulder as she walked away.

A woman in a long puffy coat stopped in front of us. "What a bitch," this new woman said to no one and it didn't make much sense, really. She laughed then, loudly, and stood watching me and Jacob, and I started feeling uncomfortable.

"Let's go," I said to Jacob.

The new woman heard me.

"No," she said, shouting a little to reach above the wind. "Stay— I like your music."

Jacob kept singing, and I tried to ignore the chick, put my instrument to my chapped lips and blew hard.

"I got a dollar," she said. She dug in a pocket, making an exaggerated show of it. She put a five-dollar bill in Jacob's bag, which he'd arranged in front of his feet, unzipped and seeded with two one-dollar bills.

The woman's eyes wandered, and she swayed and bounced out of time with our rhythm. After a while, she removed a phone from a pocket and began texting into it. After another while, a man in a pink button-down shirt and Sperry boat shoes walked up to the woman. He wore an unzipped North Face jacket over the pink shirt, and it seemed just stupid not to zip the jacket up. He looked like a guy I'd worked with, a dude who spent everything he made on clothes and jewelry and shit like that and ended up testifying against me at trial.

"What you up to, baby girl?" the dude asked the woman.

"Hey!" she shouted back. "I'm listening to music."

"Come on. Let's bounce." The guy nodded up the street.

"Uh-uh," the woman said. She shook her head and then she kept shaking it, and her hair fell over her face and she shut her eyes.

"Give 'em a buck," she said after a bit. "They're good."

"Nah, come on," the man said again.

"Fine." The chick raised her head and brushed the hair out of her eyes and stopped acting a fool. "Where'd you want to go?" She held back and didn't start walking with the guy.

"Wherever. I don't care. Let's get something to eat."

"Okay, but give these dudes something. They're cool." She gestured to Jacob's bag.

"I got no cash," the man said.

"Fuck you. You got cash." She pulled her arm away from the dude.

The guy unzipped a pocket of the jacket and took out a wallet. He pulled two one-dollar bills from it and held them out to her. She took the money and stepped over to Jacob's bag and set the bills in it.

Jacob nodded at her. She smiled, the dude pulled out his phone and stared into it, and I thought back to the days when these two fools would have been potential customers. I knew them: the privilege, the self-indulgence, the boredom. College kids with tuition-paying parents and a taste for whatever it was the products I once imported gave people who already had everything they needed. When Jacob stopped singing, I put my harmonica in my pocket.

"Let's go," I said. "We got enough."

"Naw, a couple more," Jacob said. "There's people out."

"Naw, fuck that. We got nine bucks. I'm hungry. Let's go to McDonald's."

I reached down and plucked the bills from Jacob's bag. Behind me, the woman sounded shrill when she shouted.

"You hungry? Why don't you come with us? My boyfriend, he's hungry."

"Aw, hell no." The guy looked up from his phone. He knew I could do nothing for him, had nothing to offer him. Louder, he said, "Sorry, man, no disrespect, but we gotta bounce." He took hold of the woman again.

"No, come on. We got nowhere to go. Let's meet these dudes." The chick pulled her arm away. "Come on," she said to me, "we'll buy you dinner. Where you from?"

"Texas," Jacob said. "But we been in Michigan the last couple years."

I'd had enough nonsense. "FCI Milan," I said.

"What's that?" the woman asked.

"It's a federal facility," Jacob said.

"Like a nuthouse?" She cocked her head.

"Like a prison," I said.

"That's cool." She grinned.

"Not really." I tried to catch Jacob's eye.

"Well, we'll buy you dinner," she said. "You want the Signature Room?"

The boyfriend stepped up. "We're not going to the Signature Room with these guys. Come on." Again, the pull on the arm, this one harder. The girl took a step toward the dude.

"Sorry, man. No disrespect," the guy repeated, "but she just does this shit to piss off her mom. Peace." He hitched two fingers toward me in some sort of salute.

People do a lot of things to piss off their moms. That shit used to be profitable, but I was done with all of it now, even free dinners.

"Let's get something to eat," I said to Jacob.

"With us," the girl called, pulling away from the boyfriend and returning to us, pushing the strap of a large purse back up her arm onto her shoulder. "The Signature Room."

"Sure, whatever. You're paying?" Jacob looked at her. His self-help books hadn't fixed his mindset.

"Yeah." The crazy bitch pulled two one-hundred-dollar bills out of a coat pocket and held them out. "Right here."

Jacob shrugged, picked up his bag, and shoved his guitar into it.

We followed the couple, and I watched Jacob's bag bang against his back, until the chick turned a corner to lead us into a dark building with a revolving door that made me feel weird, like it was spinning me from the windchill and noise of the street into too much emptiness and quiet. The boyfriend, who hadn't said anything while we were walking, tilted his head toward some elevators. My ears popped as we stood in the box that dragged us upward, and we all looked away from one another because we knew we didn't belong in that box together.

We didn't belong at the host stand either, and the dude at the stand looked at us when the chick asked for a table by a window. The boyfriend walked off toward the sign for the restroom.

"It's cool," the girl said to the host. "They're cool. Here, put us by the window, and here." She held out one of her one-hundred-dollar bills.

With our dirty bags, we followed the dude to a table and Jacob pulled out the chair by the aisle, so I had to take the seat by the window. I looked down to the big lake a thousand feet below and my stomach and throat felt weird. I remembered that feeling from somewhere else, maybe my sentencing hearing or something. After we sat down, the girl got right back up.

"I gotta pee. I'll be right back. If Nick comes back, tell him to get me some wine. Red."

"Sure," Jacob said.

I waited for her to make it past the host stand and the elevators and then stood up. "Let's get the fuck out of here. This is some fucked-up shit."

"You serious? No way. I'm eating a nice dinner on this bitch's dime." Jacob opened a menu.

"Seriously? That's a crazy bitch."

"Sit down," Jacob said. "The dude's coming over here."

The boyfriend, Nick, walked toward the table. I sat down. When Nick arrived at the table, he sat across from Jacob. His eyes seemed too wide. He opened a menu and held it close to his face.

"Your girlfriend told us to ask you to get her some red wine," Jacob said to him. "She went to pee."

"Sure," Nick said. "Wine. Yeah, let's get some wine."

He set his menu down and groped for the wine list, lifting and dropping the woman's menu and my menu in his search. When he picked up the list, which had been sitting by his right elbow, he looked at it like broke-ass guys look at eight balls.

"Look here, gentlemen," he said after a while. "A Cabernet Sauvignon from Shafer Vineyards: One Point Five. From Napa. I like Napa. 2014—a good year. Only $180. We'll get two bottles for the table. You ever been to Napa?"

He turned to me. Jacob hunched behind his menu.

"No," I answered.

"It's a nice place. I went there a couple years ago for a buddy's bachelor party. Got so wasted. What do you want to eat? How about the lamb chops? Or a steak? I think I'm going to have the surf and turf. We should all have the surf and turf—except Leslie won't have the surf and turf. She's a vegetarian. Pescatarian, actually. She'll have the surf, just not the turf. So she won't get surf and turf. I'll get her the scallops. So surf and turf for everyone else?"

"Sure," Jacob said. He shut his menu and put it on the plain white plate in front of him.

I shrugged.

When a waiter approached us, Nick got a little louder. He ordered the wine.

"And let's do a mushroom strudel to start. Sound good?" He looked from me to Jacob.

"All right," Jacob said.

The waiter walked off. Below us, the lake had turned the color of concertina wire with the sun setting on the other side of the building. I was looking at it when the woman—Leslie—returned. She pulled out the chair across from me. She still had her coat on, and I tried to keep my eyes on the lake as she struggled out of it.

"We've decided on surf and turf for the table and scallops for you," Nick said. "I ordered cab for the table."

"That's fine. It's pretty out, huh? You know, I'll text Megan. She should meet us here. I'll bet she's around. She should come have a drink with us. Meet our new friends. Don't you think? I'll text her."

Leslie twisted in her seat, mumbling and leaning over the back of her chair.

"Megan's laid up, remember?" Nick rolled his eyes.

Leslie untwisted, phone in her hand, and Nick faced her and the window. I was glad I was outside their conversation.

"She went in for her abortion today, remember?" Nick snorted. "She won't be around for days. I'm sure of it."

"Oh, yeah. I forgot. Maybe I should text her." Leslie looked like she was talking to the tablecloth. "I'll see if she's all right." She stared into her phone, swaying a little as she started punching her finger into the screen.

"Text her later, boo. You're being rude."

"Just lemme text her really quick." She finished with the phone and set it next to her plate. The screen reflected off the dark window. "What're your names?" She turned to look at me and Jacob and set her elbows on either side of the plate and silverware in front of her and set her chin in her hands.

"I'm Jacob. This is Neil."

"And you're from Texas?"

"Yeah, Corpus Christi," Jacob answered.

"But you were in prison?"

"For a while," Jacob said.

"Where are you going now? What brought you to Chicago?"

"We're going to Milwaukee." Jacob dug a nail into the hollow behind his right ear.

The waiter returned, held a bottle of wine out to Nick. Nick looked at the label. I watched the cars way below us. After he'd finished pouring wine into our glasses, the waiter looked at me and Jacob for too long. I turned away from the window and caught him at it, and he looked away.

"Why are you going to Milwaukee?" Leslie asked.

"Friend of ours has jobs for us there," Jacob answered.

"Well, that's perfect! We go to school in Madison," Leslie said. "We're just chilling at my mom's place this weekend. She's on a photo safari in Africa. Where'd she go again?" She turned to Nick and grabbed his arm. "Where'd she go? The name of the country? That my mom's in." She glanced at me. "He knows. He's good with remembering stuff like that." Then back to him. "Where'd she go, Nick?"

"Kenya. She's in Kenya, boo." Nick rolled his eyes again, took a long sip of wine.

I hadn't touched my glass yet. I reached for it.

"It's good, huh?" Leslie looked at me and nodded her head fast. "Sure."

The wine violated my supervised release, but I had two more days before I had to report to the probation office.

"You can stay with us if you want. At my mom's place. We'll drive you to Milwaukee on our way back to Madison tomorrow. My mom has a nice place. You can stay there. Are you guys allergic to cats? She has two cats. Nick hates cats, but he says these are okay because they don't come out much. And they don't shed much. And they're hypoallergenic. So even if you're allergic, you should be okay. It's just for the night, too. Right? It should be fine."

"Sure," Jacob said. "We're fine with cats."

The lights in the buildings around and below us were coming on, little gold squares strung over the city.

The waiter came back with the mushroom appetizer, and Nick ordered the rest of the food. The waiter poured more wine into all the glasses before he walked away. He didn't look at me. Leslie started talking about music, asked something about music, and Jacob said something to her.

Nick shook his head. "She listens to Justin Timberlake." He picked up one of the wine bottles, grinned, and took a long swig from it. His eyes had turned that familiar red. He put the bottle down, rested his forearms on the table, and leaned over toward me, forcing Leslie to sit back in her chair.

"So you guys were in prison? What for?"

"Murder," Jacob said. "Killing a couple motherfuckers."

"I thought you said it was federal. What'd you do? Kill some Indian motherfucker on a reservation?" He laughed. "My dad's an attorney. You didn't kill anyone."

He looked at me again, and below us, pocks of red spread down the lakeshore as traffic backed up.

"Cocaine," Jacob said. "A lot of cocaine. And all the shit that goes with it."

"Shit? Like what shit?"

"Like firearms in furtherance of, maintaining a drug house, supps for priors. Let's see. What else, Neil?" I didn't look up. Jacob kept running his mouth. "We went to trial, so it was a lot. The government superseded a couple a times. There were a bunch of counts."

The truth was he remembered every word of each of the indictments, every page, every charge. I knew he did. I remembered.

"How'd they catch you?"

"They pulled me over for an obstructed license plate on 94 outside Battle Creek. We were bringing a bunch of shit up from the border. Somebody dropped a dime."

"How long'd you get?"

The waiter and another guy arrived with the food. The other guy stood in the background as the waiter set plates in front of us and asked how everything looked. Jacob never answered about sentencing. He took a bite of steak right away and chewed for a long time. And then we all just ate for a while.

Leslie bobbed her head as she chewed. Nick put the empty wine bottles at the edge of the table, and the waiter took them away. Nick ordered old-fashioneds for the table.

"I gotta piss," he said after the waiter left. "Be right back."

"Do you like the food?" Leslie asked.

"Sure, it's good. Best we've had in a while," Jacob said. He was chewing and grinning and had gone even further up the it-ain't-so-bad scale.

"You want to try a scallop?" Leslie speared a scallop and held it across the table on her fork. Jacob shifted in his seat. He looked at me; I turned away.

"Here," she said, poking the fork toward him. "Just try it. It's fine. Take it." She circled the fork. "I don't bite. I like you."

Jacob glanced at me again, ran a hand through his hair. Then he sighed, and I felt him lean forward. I kept looking out the window, but I sensed him eat that scallop off her fork.

"I'm missing the party, huh?" Nick took his seat again. He spread his napkin in his lap and looked toward me. The waiter appeared with the new drinks.

"So were you like someone's bitch in prison?" Neil took his time lifting the liquor to his mouth.

"Shut the fuck up, Nick," Leslie said. "What the fuck is wrong with you?"

"It's no big thing. It happens to everybody in there." He watched me over the rim of the glass.

"No," I lied, turning from the lobster in front of me. "To be someone's bitch, I'd a had to look more like you."

Leslie snorted.

"Fuck you." Nick gave up the act with the drink and the glass.

"He's high. And he's pure cancer when he's high. Fuck him. Do you want a scallop?" Leslie held the fleshy circle out to me on her fork.

"No," I said. She put the thing back down on her plate.

"Nick, you're an asshole," she said. She picked up her phone and swiped across the screen. Nick picked up her old-fashioned and drank it.

"Look," she said. "Megan texted me back. She says she feels like shit."

"I'm sure she does," Nick said. "But she'll be ready for another trip to the Eiffel Tower in a couple days."

"Let's go. You're poison," she said. She looked out over the restaurant and must have seen the waiter. She waved.

The guy approached our table, she asked for the check, and when the dude returned, she handed him a credit card.

"My mom's," she said. She leaned toward me. "She's gonna love this."

On the street a thousand feet below the restaurant, she took hold of Jacob's arm.

"We're not far from my mom's place. It's just inland a couple blocks and like half a mile north."

The building was four stories tall and sat behind a black iron gate. When I looked up as Leslie jiggled the gate open, I knew which windows belonged to her mom's place: on the third floor, light shone into the night through glass wearing bat decals and grinning fake skeletons. The windows of a woman who'd have a daughter like this one, a daughter who would have bought from the person I'd been years ago. Standing on that street, looking up and through those windows, I remembered before, remembered selling. And then I remembered taking my boy out in a Spiderman costume—remembered that today was the day before Halloween. I shivered. Maybe it had gotten colder.

We rode to the third floor, and Leslie unlocked the condo. She fiddled with a security box to the right of the door. When I was a kid, I was good with those boxes, which later earned me some criminal-history points. A large gray cat walked up and sat in front of us and began crying.

"Robinette has anxiety issues," Leslie said. "Hang on a sec."

She turned down a hallway, and we heard her shout, "Fucking Graciella. Look at these litter boxes."

Overhead, plastic bats and skeletons and witches on brooms with weird plastic bristles bobbed. They must have been strung up with elastic thread because they bounced up and down when the dude, Nick, walked through the mess to drop onto a pink couch. He sat back and pulled a joint out of a pocket.

"Either of you got a light?" He looked at me and Jacob. "Boo," he shouted. "You got a light somewhere in here?"

Leslie returned from wherever she'd gone, wherever the dirty litter boxes were, with a gray vest-type thing she put on the squirming, howling cat. She velcroed the vest thing around the animal.

"It's her ThunderShirt," she said. She looked up at us from her knees. The cat had stopped wriggling and had flopped down next to her. "It helps with her anxiety. She has a lot of anxiety issues. And she was here alone all day. Poor Miss Robinette. It's gotten worse as she's gotten older."

"Where's a light, babe?" Nick lay across the sofa, flipping the joint back and forth between his fingers.

"I'm busy with the cat. I'll get it in a second. There's gotta be one in the kitchen. You go get it. Look in the drawer by the stove."

She stayed on the floor, petting the cat. It lay on the carpet, panting. "Take off your shoes, would you?" She kept looking at the cat, but she pointed to a wooden shelf by the door behind Jacob. A pair of high heels sat on it. They looked like they were made of black-and-white snake skin.

"Boo, you done with that cat? Get me the lighter, okay?"

I looked at Jacob. I thought about backing out the door. We could find a shelter. I wanted nothing from these people. They—the big "they," the "them" of all "these people"—had taken enough from me, just like I'd taken from them. We were square now and I was done with them. But Jacob had set his bag on the carpet and bent to untie a shoe. Another cat came around a corner and rubbed against the shoe. Nick got off the couch and walked down a hall.

"You guys can sleep in the spare salon." Leslie looked up from the gray cat, the one in the shirt, and pointed down a different hallway. "One of you can sleep in there, and then it adjoins a guest room. There are a bunch of blankets and sheets in the closet in the guest room. It's right down there. Third door on the right. You go check it out. And then we can get something to drink. You can play us some music. I'll stay here with Miss Robinette."

She picked the cat up and held it like a baby. It didn't make any noise with the shirt on. Jacob turned to me, shrugged, picked up his bag and started down the hallway Leslie had pointed toward. I put my shoes on the shelf and followed him. The hallway had paperboard gravestones on the walls, and cloth ghosts hung by their necks from the ceiling.

The guest space was all pink and red, kind of like the couch Nick had been on. The bedroom area had a big covered bed, like something from an old castle. The area next to it had a living room and then a kitchen area. It was like a separate apartment in the condo. It didn't have any of the freaky decorations in it, but it still felt fake, the way the ghosts in the hall were fake. Jacob sat down on the bed.

"Let's get the fuck outta here," I said to him. "This is fucking weird. That chick is fucked in the head and the dude's an asshole and I'm done with these fools."

"You want to sleep here or at some mission?

"A mission."

Jacob laid back on the bed. "It's nice."

"Yeah, so's not getting arrested for weed, crack, and whatever else that crazy motherfucker's got on him. I don't need these people. I don't want anything from these people. I want to bounce."

"Fuckin' relax. It's warm in here. We got a real place to sleep. We'll leave early and get a bus. Kevin'll pick us up when we get in and everything'll be fine. See what's in that closet." Jacob pointed to the closet doors.

I found a red comforter with gold horse heads on it, two red pillows, and a vibrator under a stack of sheets.

"Bitch's got bedding and a dildo in here." I snorted. "Or maybe it's Megan's." I was surprised I remembered the friend's name and then I was surprised that I kind of chuckled.

"What the fuck is wrong with you, man?" Jacob sat up. He laughed, too. "Chill. Just get your blankets and go sleep on that couch."

"You want something to drink?" Leslie stood in the doorway to the guest room. She had a bottle of vodka in one hand and a bag of weed in the other. "Nick wants to party." She held up the weed. "This stuff isn't bad. I got it from a guy from Kenosha."

"Nah, thanks, I'm good." I stood in front of the closet, holding the horse comforter and pillows.

"Sure. What else ya got?" Jacob pushed himself up from the bed and stepped over to her.

"Come see." She walked off down the hall.

I shook my head. "Dude, you gotta drop in two days."

Jacob shrugged.

"Whatever." I walked past him to the guest living room and put the pillows and comforter on the couch. I didn't take off my clothes.

We got up around four in the morning. Jacob's eyes were deep red. We got our shoes off the shelf by the door and walked out the black iron gate and found our way down to Randolph Street. I remembered it from the day before.

"We need to go that way." I flipped my head to the right, and Jacob followed me.

We crossed the river in the dark on the old metal bridge and I stopped in the middle, the water black and silent and (I was sure) very, very cold. Cold like the rest of Chicago. Cold like so many things.

For most of the ride to Milwaukee, I slept, talking myself into relaxing—Leslie and Nick and their funhouse behind us. The scales balanced. The tab square. I'd paid in years, many years, for what that world said I'd taken.

Now I could say I'd done more than look in the window. I'd stepped through the door, even slept in that world for a few hours . . . the world of mothers on African safaris and $180 wine and condos strung with safety nets I'd never had. It still felt like they'd offered it all to me—the things I'd supposedly taken, the money and the innocence. They'd offered it all for the products I'd traded them. It didn't feel like I'd cheated anyone, but that was the court's call. All I knew now was I didn't want anything from them. I'd seen it and it wasn't worth it . . . unless Kevin failed to come through with the jobs in Milwaukee.

Recompense

The candle flickered before the icon. She knelt, whispered of her work at the food pantry and homeless shelter, her efforts to pay Him back for all her sins, for all the graces she'd stolen. In the shadows, she imagined a baby, imagined hope—He would bless her once she'd made repayment.

Asmahan-Amanda

Ladies and gentlemen, welcome! Welcome to Shiraz, Chicago's favorite Persian dining experience. You're about to enjoy an evening of magical music and dance. You will experience the enchantment of our own Asmahan, direct from Cairo!"

Yes, Asmahan smoothed the skirt beneath the belt of her *bedlah, direct from Cairo.* Certainly not from Eau Claire, Wisconsin, and certainly not under the name of Amanda Phillips. And what American could name any city in old Persia? So Cairo it was—Asmahan of the Nile.

"You'll start with a taste of the traditional Egyptian wedding *zaffa,* a procession led by our Asmahan wearing a flaming candelabrum."

Because Asmahan loved weddings . . . because Asmahan didn't get pregnant at sixteen and end up with a GED and a baby-daddy who never paid child support. Because she hadn't lived with that lawyer on LaSalle for a year just to save up for new costumes and a tablet for her daughter.

"You'll see *baladi* and the *saidi,* a cane dance from Upper Egypt. And then we'll go to Turkey, and you'll bask in the intrigue of the romantic *chiftetelli* and the high spirits of *Rompi Rompi.*"

Because Asmahan had traveled the world. She had stamps in her passport from Greece and Italy, Paris and London, Shanghai and Morocco. She knew at least three languages and drank all sorts of wines. She didn't waitress at Maggiano's, and the $130 a performance Asmahan earned at Shirz didn't mean anything to her—she spent it on spa days and new shoes . . . not on cell-phone bills and quarters for the laundry and Lean Cuisines.

"Under Asmahan's spell, you'll enjoy modern Lebanese pop and Egyptian *shaabi,* with its edgy street rhythms and casual costuming. And then she'll give you the folk rhythms of the Arabian peninsula's *khaleegy,* with all that lovely hair tossing, and the *fellahi* dance of Egyptian farmers." Conspiratorially, "These farmer costumes are not so sexy."

Asmahan caught Mr. Kordestani's wink at his audience . . . because she was sharp like that. She didn't get lost in new cities or fumble around or miss little social cues. Big words didn't confuse her or make her feel dumb.

Mr. Kordestani continued beneath the too-bright lights. "But not to worry because you'll get a nice costume again for the drum solo."

Asmahan didn't like the baggy peasant *fellahi* dress or the silly pom-pom'ed headpiece she wore with it. She hated the *melaya leff* dress and its giant black shroud for the Alexandrian number. But Mr. Kordestani wanted folk pieces and "art" in his shows, not just cabaret shimmies. Whatever that meant. And Asmahan would never complain about such directorial choices—she was a professional. She had, after all, danced for audiences nationwide . . . at the Michigan Renaissance Festival in Holly and the Northern Indiana International Festival in Mishawaka.

Asmahan's life meant something.

The *oud* rose, softly. . . .

"So without further ado, I give you the Goddess of the Nile, Asmahan!"

Falls

"Whatever."

The door slammed behind him.

And I suddenly knew the feeling of going over Niagara Falls in a barrel, of falling from the deck of a ship in some black night of storm and waves, of being Summer executed by Fall's angry rain year after year.

Of falling in love too late. Or something like that.

Queen

Our building sits on Randolph Street, so cabs are never in short supply. But Yvonne's recent love affair with Lyft has left me standing outside the building, staring at my phone, watching the little car icon that represents Daniyal in a blue Nissan Versa. It creeps toward me and makes a stiff, perfectly ninety-degree left turn. He's getting close.

The little icon exhumes some lost, superannuated memory. As I stare at that tiny car, I'm fifteen again and pulling from beneath the Christmas tree a bright red package with a green bow and a tangle of white, hand-cut snowflakes tied to and hanging from it. After tearing away the paper, I realize my father has made me the first boy in the neighborhood to own Pong. I am happy in a way I have not been happy in a long, long time.

And then I am not. Then I am simply on Randolph Street again.

"Where are you going, sir?" Daniyal asks after the icon arrives in front of my building and I open the door to the Versa.

"Two-fifty-one East Huron. Northwestern Memorial. I thought the phone told you that. It doesn't tell you that?"

"Oh, it tells me. I just like to double-check. Make sure we're all on the same page."

"Oh. Makes sense." I fumble to buckle the seatbelt in a backseat too small to accommodate any properly nourished adult. "It's my first time trying this—Lyft. My wife told me to try it since it's such a short trip. She loves this stuff and keeps pushing me to learn to use it. Says I'll save a fortune."

"Perhaps." He looks at me in the rearview mirror. "Would you like music?" He reaches for the stereo. "What do you like?"

"Oh, I'm fine without it. A little quiet is okay." I inhale canned pine forest and the solitude I interrupted when I slid into the vehicle.

The light turns red and we sit in the blue car in the darkness. Daniyal stares straight out the windshield, his hands at ten and two. I watch a woman on a bike rock back and forth beside my window, her bright red jacket pricking my eyes but also taking me back to that wrapping paper and Pong all those long, long, lost and gone years ago.

The light changes, and Daniyal pulls across the intersection. I shift in my confines.

Yvonne has texted: *You make it into a Lyft*. When she texts, she feels she can omit punctuation. That bothers me.

Yes, I reply. I add, *Very small car.* I want her to know I'm okay for now.

A black hatchback has replaced the bike. In its back window, it has a sticker that reads *Crazy Cat Lady*. I am relieved that silent Daniyal picked me up and not someone with a sticker like that.

"Is the temperature okay? Would you like some more heat?" Daniyal glances up at the mirror again.

"Oh, no. Not at all. Perfectly fine back here. Thank you."

The river gets closer. It should take only three or four minutes to get to the hospital. If everything goes as the doctor said, I should be home by eight. Yvonne will have some wine for me. Maybe she'll let me nip at the Macallan. That nice twenty-one-year-old single malt Marcus gave me for my birthday. I'll feel better after a drink or two.

"Where are you from, Daniyal?" My voice lifts the weight of the car's interior off me a little. "Did you grow up in the city?"

"Oh, no. I'm from Sidon. Lebanon."

"Sidon? I was in Beirut in '82."

Another memory uncurls from its place of slumber.

"Just a wet-behind-the-ears second lieutenant out of Annapolis." I shake my head at this second bit of detritus for the evening.

"It was a bad time," Daniyal says.

Daniyal turns right and we stop. We are sitting in a pool of darkness, with red brake-light water lilies all around us.

"I'm sorry. The bridge is up."

"It appears so, doesn't it? Is it supposed to be up at this hour?"

"I don't think so. I haven't seen it up like this at night, at least not this time of year, that I can remember."

Maybe I should have put some of that Macallan in a flask, but I certainly wasn't expecting this.

"There were things I liked about it over there," I say to the window, watching a pair of women on the sidewalk with shopping bags in their hands and a boy of about ten walking between them. "I liked the music. I listened to a lot of the local music, bought records and brought them back with me. It was good stuff."

Beside us, on the sidewalk, sits a row of dark cubes topped by a sign that reads *Newspapers*. I can't remember the last time I held an actual newspaper. Oh, the terror Pong kicked off.

"I remember listening to a woman singer," I say, trying to remember the name. "Her name was something like Fairuz. I liked her. A lot. Very pretty voice."

"You know Fairuz?" Daniyal's eyes look back from the mirror again.

"Yes. I liked her. I remember a song—" I have to stop and think, as with recalling the woman singer's name.

I turn from the window and the landscape of the obsolete newspaper rack to place my hand against my jaw and temple. "It was called—" It takes me a minute. At first, I can only see that circle bouncing back and forth between the Pong paddles. Then I am outside a bar in the hinterlands of Anne Arundel County. And then I remember.

"It was called '*Habaytak Bisayf*.' Am I saying that right?"

"'*Habaytak Bisayf*'? Yes, perfectly. That is one of my favorite songs. They say she has the voice of an angel." Now it's Daniyal's smile that fills the mirror.

"Yes, that song is very beautiful."

This was supposed to be a five-minute ride. Yet somehow it has taken me back to Lebanon, and I am a twenty-two-year-old kid again, and it's all so, so far back: back before all the nonsense, the anger, the infidelities big and small on both sides; long before Yvonne and the occasional description of "second wife." Back before what they call success, and long, long before unrecognized, undiagnosed *anythings* lying in wait in brain tissue and heartbreaks. Back closer to the happiness of Pong and love songs and memories of home. I am newly wed to Margaret—azure-eyed Margaret of quick temper and languid seduction—and full of hope and plans.

Outside the Versa, a young man balances on one of those so-called hoverboards, bags of what I think are groceries slung over his shoulders. I remember how I thought it romantic and gallant to carry Margaret's picture in my pocket through Beirut, how that first kiss tingled and breathed when I returned home, how I told her she had seen the Levant from my pocket.

"What other music do you listen to?" I ask Daniyal.

"Queen. I love Queen. We will rock you!"

"Freddie Mercury. He was talented. Creative."

"Oh, yes," Daniyal says.

"I should have listened to more Queen in the eighties. It's good stuff." I sigh. "Would've been better than all that Lebanese music I brought back. My daughter got old enough to put those records on, and now she dances at restaurants down in South Bend. If it'd been Queen, maybe she would've played volleyball or tennis."

"Your daughter dances to Lebanese music?"

"Yes." I sigh a second time and shake my head. "She performs dinner shows at Middle Eastern restaurants. She's going to school down there but spends all my money on custom-made costumes from Turkey and traveling all over to take dance workshops. She dances to that woman Fairuz's songs. I've seen her, but I don't like it. Something about it makes me uncomfortable.

"Her stepmom loves it, though. Sabrina—my daughter—she didn't get along with Yvonne—my wife—at first. Sabrina was upset I'd remarried. But it was time. Now the two of them are right as rain. Yvonne drives down there and takes the dance workshops Sabrina teaches. Yvonne's all into the whole silly thing too."

I hear Daniyal chuckle.

"Would you like to hear '*Habaytak Bisayf*'? I have it here." He touches his phone.

"Sure."

"*Be ayam el bard, be ayam el sheti.*" That voice fills the Versa. "*We el raseef bohayra, we el sharea gharee'a.*"

"I know it's a love song," I say. "Someone told me once what it means, but I don't remember. What does it mean?"

"It's winter. Cold. And the sidewalks are flooded like a lake," Daniyal answers. "This girl is waiting for him. He told her to wait, but he has gone away. He's forgotten her, but she is pining for him. She loved him in the summer and waited for him in the winter. His eyes are summer. Hers are winter. And their reunion, 'oh my love,' is beyond summer and beyond winter."

He clears his throat.

"A stranger passes and gives her a message," he continues translating. Then another cough. "The boy wrote it with his tears. The message, the letters of it, were lost. The days passed. The years made them strangers. And winter erased the letters in the message."

He tries to clear his throat yet again, blows his nose on a tissue from the colored, patterned box sitting on the passenger seat, and then lifts a bottle of water from that seat. The voice from the phone fades and then rises again in a new rhythm with a new story.

"Sad," I say.

"Yes, very sad."

"It sounds sad even just listening to it—not even knowing the words."

"It was my wife's favorite song," Daniyal says. "She sang along, and I always had to tell her to stop—that I would never leave her or write her messages without letters in them. But she would laugh and keep singing and dance in circles. Not like your daughter." He tries to laugh. "Just in our home."

He pauses, takes another sip of water from the bottle. "But once she danced on the beach. Did you ever go to Sidon?"

"Yes, actually, I did once."

"You saw the castle on the sea?"

"Yes, the crusaders' fortress. Yes, I remember that." I see myself, a young Marine officer, watching the sun set behind a medieval castle on the Mediterranean, Margaret's picture in my pocket.

"You know what, Daniyal, would you mind putting on a little more heat back here now?"

"Of course."

"Thank you."

"The castle is beautiful, is it not?" Daniyal's hands rub up and down the steering wheel, fingers flexing in and out.

"Yes, very impressive."

"We were there one evening when we were kids. Just married. Young and happy, and she danced and sang. She danced on the sand. She had her arms flung out." Daniyal imitates a gesture of abandon.

He takes another drink of water.

"She—my wife—had long black hair, like the sky over the sea at night."

I see him turn and look out at the walk along the river and at the bridge. I know he sees his wife dancing on the beach some long-lost night ago. He wheezes against the nagging grip on his throat and blows his nose again. I pretend not to notice why.

"We—we had the *Ginnaz*, the prayers, and then the bread forty days after that," he says, eyes and attention on the other side of the window, of the world. "I pray she is with our Holy Mother."

The Versa has warmed up, perhaps too much now, and the only thing I can say is "I'm sorry for your loss." The tone of my voice is too low.

"Oh, no. This is life. Death is a part of life."

"She was very young?" I don't know why I ask.

"Twenty when she was struck and went into the coma," he replies. "We had gone to Beirut because she was having some sickness we could not explain. We thought we could do better at a hospital in Beirut, and my uncle told us to come stay with his family there. But then the Israeli bombing started. You know how it was. You were there. And she was walking one day—"

He robs the box of another of its white squares of Kleenex. "Excuse me."

"Oh, no. And you don't have to—"

"No, it is good to remember," he insists. "She had just turned twenty-two when she left us. I sat with her every day. We read together: poems and scripture and stories. She loved to read."

He smiles into that mirror.

"And I sang to her. I sang her Fairuz. Every day, we were together. My uncle took care of me, and I went to the hospital every day."

The block has returned to his throat.

"She never woke up after the bomb. But it didn't matter. I just wanted to sit beside her. The last day, that afternoon, I was reading to her, and you know . . . ." He looks at me in the mirror, waits to catch my eyes with his. "She squeezed my hand. Truly. I was holding her hand and she squeezed mine tightly and then she was gone. I pray God lets me take that memory to my own deathbed."

He crosses himself, touching his right shoulder and then his left.

The Nissan is quiet.

Outside the windows, we see the bridge start to lower.

"Yvonne is Catholic," I blurt out. "I'll tell her to say a prayer. It is good to pray for the dead. What was your wife's name?"

"Marina." He inhales and exhales a few times. "Thank you."

"Yvonne will light a candle on Sunday."

"Thank you."

The bridge finds its mate from the other side of the river, and the traffic loosens, the knot of cars released to flow and rediscover their rhythm.

From the river, it is only a few minutes to the hospital. Daniyal pulls up in front of the doors to which I direct him.

"Wait," he says as I begin to thank him for the ride. "Are you ill? Are you here because you are ill? I'll park and walk in with you."

He presses the button on his dash to activate his hazard lights.

"You shouldn't go in alone. No one should go to a hospital alone." He turns the car off and opens his door.

"Oh, no, thank you, but I'm only going in to attend to some paperwork," I tell him. "No need to worry, but I do appreciate your kindness. Thank you."

"Okay then. Good luck, and listen to Fairuz once in a while, and then to Freddie Mercury and Queen." He smiles into the mirror a last time, and I catch him catching something in my face.

"Here, sir." He reaches for his box and hands me a tissue I hadn't realized I needed. He keeps looking. "Here," he repeats and hands me the box.

"Thank you." I grope to connect with the box and take it from him without looking up from my other hand resting on the inside of the car door. "Thank you for the ride. And the music."

I shut the door of the Nissan and approach the hospital entrance, the windows in the gray building amber in the night. I haven't been here in a long time, and maybe the light of the windows isn't amber. Maybe it's marigold or saffron. Regardless, it's the color of a world I have avoided for a long, long time. But this is the last time.

On the other side of the windows, I follow the doctor's white coat down a hallway. Margaret lies in the bed, as she has for nineteen months. The ball of the world has bounced back and forth between the paddles of man's machinations, but nothing true or real has altered the monochrome, the antiseptic scent of affliction, the simple shapes on the screen of existence. The ventilator makes Margaret's chest rise and fall. The doctor hands me a clipboard and I nod and sign. The Kleenex box dangles in my left hand as I pass the board back; I don't want to use the tissues, so I don't try to speak. I am sure I am gone and out of the building before Margaret is gone. It is very dark now and I walk toward St. Clair Street.

On Sunday, I'll ask Yvonne to light two candles. She'll understand.

On St. Clair, I flag down a cab for the trip home.

*

His profile had read entrepreneur. She didn't expect him to own a delivery truck. But the evening was warm and the music from the bar reminded her of home.

Her profile had read thirty-eight years old. He hadn't expected that to mean forty-five. Oh, well. They had Goose Island on tap, and *it* had been a while, so he decided to stick it out till the end.

St. Peter's Salsa Club

Helen hadn't thought too much about death. Regardless, she wouldn't have expected this. St. Peter met her at the pearly gates in pointy-toed dance shoes and a vest the color of the inside of an abalone shell. He welcomed her with the politest smile she'd ever seen, but he didn't seem too focused on the Scripture passages she offered or the fact she'd gotten Last Rites just before "arriving." He simply asked what she felt she'd missed in life.

The question took her by surprise. She thought she'd lived a good life. Eighty-six years of being a good daughter, a good student, a good postal carrier, a good wife (she was excited to hear she'd be with Roger again!), a good mother (and she was happy to hear she wouldn't be seeing the boys anytime soon—they had many more years in front of them down there).

"I guess I just wish I'd learned to dance," she finally stammered. "And maybe I wish I'd traveled more." Two trips to Orlando and a trip to San Diego weren't really much over the course of eighty-six years after all. Vacations had always been to the cottage.

St. Peter turned, lifted a silver cylinder from a cloud and let it float in front of Helen. Next he pulled two sanded wooden dowels from another cloud, each rod less than a foot long. He tapped them a few times:

X X X . . . X X
X X X . . . X X

Then he tapped the still-floating cylinder with one of the sticks, explaining as he did so, "These are claves. For salsa music."

A diamond mist sprayed out of the cylinder, blinded Helen in glitter and sparkles . . . and she was on a beach outside Havana.

Celia Cruz cried out, *"No hay que llorar! Que la vida es un carnaval."* Helen surprised herself by understanding: There's no need to cry. Life is a carnival.

In Santo Domingo, she heard Yoskar Sarante sing that he had no luck in love. A lovely young man spun her across the dance floor in the step-step-step-tap of *bachata* till she was dizzy—but not quite. Maybe you can't get dizzy once you cross over.

In Vienna, she waltzed beside the Blue Danube. In Luxor, she wore a purple-spangled dress and wielded a cane overhead to the dum-tek-dum-dum-tek of the heavy, playful *saidi*. In Chuuk, she donned a torn white t-shirt and ripped denim cutoffs to twirl to music that sounded a little like the pulse of the *Tinikling* bamboo stick dance she discovered in Kawayan, south of Manila—but without the bamboo dance's strong ¾ time. In Vegas, she cried when Tupac sang "Dear Mama," and she cried again sitting beside Bruddah Iz, watching a rainbow form over Diamond Head. But it was all joy lindy hopping with Frankie Manning at the Savoy.

All joy.

In 4/4 time.

*

On the other side of the horizon
lies happiness, I'm sure.
It's the color of a mango's skin
and smells like the day after Christmas
when the tree is still up and the house is very quiet
and someone has put a new candle out to burn.

On the other side of the horizon
no one jerks awake at four in the morning,
and if they do, they can fall back asleep right away anyway

Because they are happy
And the happiness tastes the way a bar of raspberry-scented soap
should taste but of course doesn't

But how do you get there
to that place where you don't want to lie

About how you are?

And does the other side of the horizon
make the same sound as the other side of tomorrow if you slip and
accidentally step on it. . . .
And will it forgive you if you do that? Slip like that and step on it and
make it make a sound?
Will it still feel like that oft-cited
(and well worn-out)
satin edge of the blanket you had when you were a kid
if you slip and step on it?
Because it was an accident, after all,
. . . in the end,
not something you could help
Or stop,
Right?

Hello?

Maybe the lights did it: stripes of flashing, swirling red and blue overhead. Maybe those lights wiped away all the memories. Because before that night at your place, before all the cops pulled up and the lights started swirling, you could remember what your mom's voice sounded like. But ever since then, you haven't been able to hear it in your head, in your memories. You can't hear her saying, "I'm proud of you," or— Well, you'll stop before you get all stupid here.

Your turn at the phone comes. Lift the receiver. Three bucks for fifteen minutes. That's everything you made yesterday, but who's counting? You've got time. Lots of time. Day after day after day. You dial. The prison phone recording plays in your ear. You wait.

You know your mom told you Ray was "bad news." You know she told you to stay away from him. But you can't remember how she sounded when she said it.

The phone recording finishes and the ringing starts.

The first ring.

Was it the drinking? You were pretty drunk when you met Ray at that party near campus. Everyone was drunk. People were having a good time. You were having a good time. What did Ray say to you? You can't remember. See? It's all gone: your mom's voice, Ray's voice, even the judge saying "seven years in the custody of the Bureau of Prisons." You know they said things, but you can't remember how those things *sounded*. Anyway, Ray said something about your eyes. You know you blushed. Because you were like that. You were a good girl. Hell, you'd never even seen cocaine before that party. Maybe if you hadn't been drinking. . . .

The second ring.

Everyone said Ray was so hot. Even Mom acknowledged that. She said, "Hey, I know he's physically attractive, but there's more to life than that. You've gotta think." The thing is: You did think. You thought about whether to let him keep that shit in your closet. You didn't just say yes. You debated with yourself first. But it was only for a couple weeks. And you were careful. You didn't look in the bags. It's like you told the cops: You didn't know what was in there. You didn't know anything.

A third ring.

Well, okay, you knew about the gun. And really, that's where you fucked up. You should never have let him put the gun in the hamper. That was a dumb-ass move. And okay, you weren't thinking then. You admitted that, too: You were high when he came over with the gun, high when you told him, "all right, Boo, but only for a couple days," high when he—whatever. Why are you even thinking about that now? But you weren't high when he testified against you at trial. You remember that at least. He copped that plea and flipped. The lawyer Mom paid for warned you about that. Mom didn't hear it all when it went down; she didn't go to your trial.

You're at the fourth ring.

And you wonder why you're doing this. It's been three years, four months, two weeks, four days since they arrested you. It felt weird— ironic?—the arrest did. The first time you wore handcuffs, Ray brought them over with an eightball and you had your panties off before he'd even closed the curtains. So actually getting cuffed, by cops, because of him, made you think about your English professor's discussion of irony when you read—aw, fuck, what was that dude's name? Guy de? Never mind.

Your throat tightens.

The ringing has stopped. So someone has picked up. Because if it had just gone to voicemail, the call would be over, but it's not over. The prison recording must be telling someone that "this is a call from a federal prison." It's a long recording, you know that. It warns people about scams and how to block calls, and you remember how Ginny deleted Ray from your phone twice and even called your mom and told her you were partying too much. You ended up deleting and blocking Ginny, and didn't you post something on her Facebook wall? Did you really put "fuck you, bitch"—because that still doesn't seem like you, even if you were high a lot back then. Do people even use Facebook anymore?

Is the recording still going? Is it really that long? Is it— And then you remember. That's how she sounds:

"Hello?"

*

When I was a kid, I dreamed of magic wardrobes, of epic worlds behind enchanted doors. Sometimes, I still think of those worlds hidden behind ordinary closets and coatracks, dream of them. Mostly, I think about them when I've stacked my tray high with dirty plates and mostly-empty water glasses . . . when I've crumpled the discarded napkins and stuffed them under the silverware on the tray. I think of silly things like that as I back through the kitchen door and dump the stack of flatware for the guy washing dishes to sort.

362 Pounds of Copper or 900 Dead Presidents

The knock on the side of my boat does not surprise me. Once I sent that text, I knew she'd be over.

"Come on down," I shout. I mute the TV in anticipation of the festivities.

She slides the hatch back and lifts the boards out of the companionway. She backs down the ladder, giving me a good view of that ample backside—to no effect.

"Did you go?"

"Where?" I watch a perky blonde woman gesture at three kids seated in front of cereal bowls on the screen.

"The doctor." She sits down on the settee and looks up at the pantomime. "Did you talk to them?"

"I didn't go to the doctor."

"Did you at least call?"

"Nope."

She pulls her phone out of her back pocket. I turn the TV's sound back on. A talking head complains about Trump. I change the channel.

"My sister is such a bitch. Look what she posted on Facebook." She holds her phone out to me.

"Pammy, you're too old for that shit. Who cares what your sister put on Facebook?"

"You see? That's the whole problem. You think like an old man, so things perform like an old man. I'm not going to give in like that. I'm young at heart."

"Pammy, you ain't been young at anything since Ford was in office."

"I don't know why you gotta be like that. I shouldn't waste my time comin' over here. I shouldn't waste my time on you. I don't know why I even care about all this."

"Me neither. Go back to your boat and your knitting."

"You're an asshole."

She gets off the settee and climbs back up the ladder, sliding the boards back in the companionway and pulling the hatch closed, burying me in the little tomb of my boat. It probably will be my tomb, too. I'll die in a few years and someone will complain to the harbormaster about the smell on dock number eleven and they'll find me down here, the cat sitting next to me—probably taking bites out of me. My kids won't care. I just hope my daughter will come get the cat and take care of it.

The hatch slides open again.

"Barry, you gotta call the doctor. Call the doctor and they'll refer you to a urologist and then you'll just go in and get a prescription, and then it'll all be good. You'll be happy. I'll be happy. I'll make you so happy. Just call."

"Pammy, don't talk like that out there for every g-d fool walkin' by on the dock to hear. Come down here if you want to talk." I mute the TV again.

"I got needs, Barry," she says as she backs down the ladder for her encore performance of *Piss Me Off on a Tuesday Afternoon.*

"I'm not going to talk about it anymore." I turn the TV up.

She sits on the settee watching the talking heads.

"You know what'd be real romantic? Let's go down to that hotel in Freeport. Across the street from the Mexican restaurant? Rooms ain't much. I think the sign said twenty-two a night last time I drove by—I was down at that marina in Freeport about a month ago to wash a bunch of boats and do some teak work. Made two hundred and seven-y bucks all in a day. Well, anyway, on the drive back up, I came by way of 288 and drove by that motel and they had a sign out: twenty-two bucks a night. And they're right by that Mexican restaurant. You could take me down there next time you get your check. We'll have a nice weekend. We'll eat dinner at that restaurant. I think it's called San Miguel's, ain't it? And you could drive me to Surfside and we could sit on the beach. I'll wear somethin' real nice for you."

"I'll take you to that motel if you want, and I'll take you to the beach if you want. I got no complaints with that. I get my check in two Wednesdays. Then you just tell me when you wanna go."

"Well, okay then. That'll be real nice."

We sit there like that for a while. Pam kinda cocks her head when she watches TV and sometimes I wonder if it don't hurt her neck to sit like that. Her phone vibrates.

"I'm gonna go," she says after looking at it. "Mimi's gonna go clean some boats on the broker docks. Says she'll gimme sixty bucks to come over give her a hand."

"You do that."

That night, I have dinner up at the pavilion. John from dock two offers me some enchiladas he made and we sit in the covered pavilion and it ain't too hot and we watch boats coming in and out of the channel. We don't talk too much, but he says "it's a nice night" maybe three or four times. Then my phone beeps.

"I made us a reservation," the text says.

I shut the phone.

"What's that?" John asks.

"Nothin'. Pam's just all actin' up because she wants some sorta romantic getaway. Wants me to take her down to Freeport. You know when you drive in down there on 288? You know that old shithole on the left? The motel? Yeah, she says it's only twenty-two bucks a night and she wants me to take her down there for the weekend and over to Surfside and to that shitty Mexican restaurant there. Been watchin' too much Oprah or somethin'. Is Oprah still on?"

"I dunno." John shrugs. "You don't wanna do it?"

"Nah, I'll do it. I just don't want all this nonsense idea about some romantic weekend. I'm too old for all that bullshit."

After we finish eating, I take the blue plastic plate he brought my enchiladas over on and I wash it in the public bathhouse. I wipe it and the fork dry and return them to John, and we walk over to his old Hunter and sit in the cockpit and drink a couple Keystones.

"You wanna work tomorrow?" he asks me after his second beer.

"Sure."

"Let's go to Joe Lee's around about seven for dinner—that gives us pleny o' time to eat. They don't close till eight. And then we'll start at the Home Depot. We'll hit Home Depot and Target and then go over to Aldi's and Walmart, and then we'll see how we're feelin'."

"Okay," I say. "Sounds fine to me."

"I'll meet you in the parking lot at six forty-five. I'll drive. I put new tires on the truck a couple weeks ago and it drives real nice now."

The next evening, I meet John and we get boudain at Joe Lee's, and then we drive toward the sprawl that houses Home Depot and Target, Chik-fil-A and Taco Cabana. It's dark, and it's fall, so it's not too hot, and no one's around when we pull behind the Home Depot.

"I meant to ask you at dinner: Pam still harpin' on you all havin' that romantic getaway?" John unbuckles his seatbelt and looks around the lot.

"Yeah, I saw her today doin' laundry. She said she'd bought some new dress for 'our weekend together.'" I open my door and get out of the truck. John has flashlights behind the seat of the cab and I pull two out.

"And you know what else she tells me?" I latch the seat back into place and shut the truck door. "She tells me that shithole motel's called Dreamer's Motel and that that's perfect for us 'cause we're dreamers— 'cause we don't live like other people and we live on the sea."

John snorts.

"'Hell,' I said to her, 'we ain't no dreamers—we're broke ass and we live in a watery mobile-home park.' And ain't that the truth." I lead the way over to the wooden enclosure that hides the dumpsters.

"Well, we're already off to a good start. Look at that. See? Maybe we is dreamers or gifted or somethin'." John points at a stack of old pallets piled next to the enclosure.

We carry the pallets to the truck and stack them in the bed. Eight of 'em—and not in bad condition. At three bucks a pop, we are off to a good start.

The enclosure isn't locked and we let ourselves in.

"You wanna do the honors tonight? Since you're a dreamer an' all?" John looks at me.

"Aw, hell." It's always hard to motivate, but I agree and step into the stirrup of John's interlaced fingers. Inside the dumpster, I sort through garbage bags, cardboard, scraps of wood, and various glass and plastic items.

"It don't smell too bad out here," John says. "That's somethin'."

"Not so hot. That helps," I say.

I can feel a bunch of soda cans in a bag, so I toss it out to John. "Here, see what you can find in here," I say, swinging the bag over the dumpster's edge to him. "Feels like cans."

I hear him tear open the bag and drop cans onto the concrete.

Toward the bottom of the mess, I find a vein: bent, dinged, and hacked copper piping.

"Bingo!"

"Whaddya got?" John hisses.

"Copper."

"Whee doggies."

Being careful not to bang the pipe on the metal dumpster, I hand lengths of it out to John. He takes care not to clang it around or drop it. We keep our voices low.

"Lemme see what else we got," I say after handing the last pieces to him.

There are three torn boxes of old plumbing fixtures—things people probably brought in as examples of what they were replacing and then discarded after buying the proper new fixtures. When I'm satisfied she's tapped out, I crawl out of the dumpster and John helps me drop to the ground.

"Not a bad start," he says.

We retrieve a couple plastic crates from the bed of the truck and dump the junk into them.

"Maybe Pam's right. Maybe you is a dreamer—got some magic touch tonight."

I grunt.

"You know, she may be on to somethin' with her whole idea," John continues. "I saw this thing on Twitter the other day 'bout people called Freegans. It's peoples that recycle and don't buy new shit and reduce consumerism. It's a real thing."

"You shittin' me, right?" I look across the bed of the truck to him as I wedge a plastic crate between the truck bed and the stack of pallets.

"No, it's a real thing," he repeats. "We're Freegans. We're helping to combat rampant consumerism that's destroying the environment." I know he's reading back in his mind whatever crap he saw on the Twitter.

"And I'm a flyin' mouse what takes rainbow shits. We're dumpster divers, John. And I wouldn't be divin' in no dumpster if I had any money to consume with."

"You're short sighted, Barry. Pam's right. You should take that vacation with her. Maybe she'll help you to find your inner potential."

After I snort and roll my eyes, I get into the truck.

"Your turn at Target," I tell John.

Because of the Starbucks and food concession in this Target and the grocery section, this dumpster always offers an olfactory feast the Home Depot dumpster cannot match. John hesitates before he steps into my hands for the spring up into the receptacle.

"Come on, Freegan, jump in and live your dream," I urge him.

He gives me a look and I chuckle.

Once in the metal shell, he starts rummaging and then tosses out two busted floor fans, a space heater missing its front cover, and a box of just-expired canned green beans. The beans are the french-cut kind.

"I'll keep these," I whisper over the edge of the bin. "I like the french-cut ones. I sauté 'em up with olive oil and black pepper. They're real nice like that."

"Well, look at this!" John's arm extends up from the morass with an extension cord. The sheath has torn near the plug end and bare wires protrude. "It's a lucky night for a couple of old Freegan dreamers." He drops the cord toward me.

Aldi's trash compound yields four large boxes of expired fish-oil bottles, a case of expired Mozartkugel, a crate of muesli in damp boxes but with intact inner plastic bags, and nets of really soft oranges. I'm glad more American's don't appreciate the finer things of European cuisine—I've learned to love Mozartkugel and can get it almost monthly from behind Aldi's. At Walmart, we find two dozen boxes of size-twelve black-canvas mules that appear from the shape of their left toe boxes to be seconds. We also retrieve four car batteries abandoned in a corner of the parking lot. It baffles me that people just throw money away like this.

"Let's take a swing through Dickinson," I suggest when we've exhausted the supply of dumpsters.

"'Kay," John agrees, and the lark pays off when we turn right onto 646. In a ditch on the left-hand side of the road lies an old dryer. John pulls onto the shoulder and we scoot across 646.

"Look at that. Someone's smilin' on us tonight." John rubs his palms on his jeans.

"Here, you take that side." I point John into position.

"Aw, shit, my knees," I croak when we lift the thing.

"Come on, brother, we got this," John encourages as we waddle back across the road to the truck. We drop the appliance near the tailgate and I heft myself into the truck bed and start rearranging crates and pallets to make room for it.

"I'll betcha we make over a hundred bucks from tonight," John estimates, as I pull and he pushes the dryer up over the tailgate.

"Could be," I agree.

At the marina, we cover our haul with a tarp and head to the bathhouse to shower. When I fall asleep next to the cat, I'm not thinking about Pam or the Dreamer's Motel or urologists.

In the morning, John has an oversized stockpot hanging off the cooktop of his old Chris Craft Commander, which has two busted Cummins diesels down below that haven't run in decades.

As is part of the ritual of coming aboard the craft, I ask him why we don't haul the old engines out and scrap them.

"I'll get 'em runnin' again someday and then she'll really be somethin' to see. I'll sell the old girl for a fortune and buy a condo up around Shoreacres."

"The hell you will," I respond.

I look around the boat and then tell John I'll go out to the truck and start cutting electrical cords off the appliances. When I return with the coil of cords, the water's boiling and I drop the things into the pot. It won't take too long for the sheaths to get nice and soft and then I'll strip the copper bare and we can take all the metal to the scrapyard and the shoes to the guy we know with the junk shop in League City. The food items I'll split with John and we'll share some around the docks with people like Pam.

The problem is she starts in on me when I offer her green beans, fish oil, oranges, and German cereal.

"Sure I'll take some, but you gotta call the doctor. Right now, Barry. You got time for all this, you got time to go get yourself checked out. You can't put this off—it ain't fair to me. You don't fix this and I'll have no choice. I'll go on that eHarmony or Match or Plenty o' Fish and find a man who'll love me *and* take care of my needs. Because I know you loves me, Barry, but you ain't takin' care of me, honey. Not by ignorin' this."

"Whatever." I hand the food over the stern of her Catalina and amble down the dock to continue my largesse.

On John's Chris Craft, the cords are ready when I return and I get to scraping, revealing the copper that's as good as gold to us.

"I been thinkin'," John says, and instinct alerts me I won't like his next words. "I don't know all the ins and outs of what's goin' on with you and Pam, but you know, Barry, you're a stubborn man. You gotta take her more seriously. That's all I'm goin' to say on the matter, but if she's tellin' you she needs somethin,' well, she's doin' the right thing by communicatin' her needs and you need to listen. Do as she says. And take her down south to that Dreamer's Motel. It ain't a bad place. You'll have a nice time. She's a good woman. You need to appreciate that."

"I come here to strip wire, John, not for Dr. Phil."

"See, that's your problem."

After we strip all the wire, sort the brass, copper, and aluminum, show our IDs at the scrapyard, and sell the shoes for fifty cents a pair in League City, John and I split our proceeds. And after a few more days of fighting a war on two fronts—Pam and John—which even Hitler would tell you you can't win when you have to fight on two fronts—I use twenty bucks of the money to cover my Medicare copay at the clinic. It isn't—pardon the pun—hard to get the referral to the urologist, and once I'm there, the nurse is good to look at, though that don't change my diagnosis. The doc forks over a prescription and I make my way to the Walgreens.

At the pharmacy counter, a woman with smooth skin and dark hair takes the prescription from me and tells me to come back in forty-five minutes. I drive back to the boat and watch Judge Judy order a couple punk kids to pay for some stereo equipment they claim their buddy gave them as an "investment" in their rap careers. The phone rings and a recording tells me my prescription is ready for pick up.

At the Walgreens, a lady holding a baby with a Styrofoam helmet on its head stands in front of me in line. It takes her a while to find the prescriptions in her purse and hand them over to the same pretty broad who took mine earlier. Then the baby-holding woman has a bunch of questions that the pharmacy woman tells her to save for the pharmacist, who'll help her when the prescriptions are ready for pick up.

"I can help you now," the dark-haired woman calls to me from her side of the counter after she's sent the mom and helmet-baby away.

"Prescription for Barry Hart. Pick up," I say to her. I fish my wallet out of my back pocket and open it to dig out a twenty.

"Let me go and get the pharmacist for you," she says.

She returns with the pharmacist.

"Have you taken this medicine before?" the pharmacist asks me.

"Nope," I reply, "never had a need."

"Well, do you understand it? Do you have any questions?"

"Nope, doc explained everything to me. Think I'm good."

"Well," the pharmacist says, "if you have any questions, you can consult the sheet included in the package for you or call us. We're happy to help."

The dark-haired woman punches keys on her cash register.

"That's nine hundred today." She smiles.

I am holding the twenty out to her. I look up from the brochure entitled "Healthy Aging" sitting beside the register.

"Excuse me?" I pull back my hand with the twenty-dollar bill and stuff the double sawbuck in my pocket.

"It'll be nine hundred dollars today, sir. For the thirty-pill supply."

"Nine hundred American dollars? Not like pesos or something? Nine hundred dollars?"

"Yes, sir. Nine hundred dollars." The woman tries to keep smiling.

"Nine hundred dollars for some pills to gimme a stiffy?"

"Um, yes. Nine hundred dollars." I am trying her smiling endurance.

"Well, that ain't gonna work."

"Oh," she says, "well, what would you like me to do, sir? Would you like me to cancel the transaction?"

"I'd like you to break up with my old lady because I sure as hell don't wanna deal with her. And cancel my reservations at the Dreamer's Motel because she's dreamin' to think I'm gonna pay some nine hundred dollars for a bunch a pills."

Back on the boat, the cat jumps into my lap and we listen to a pundit harping about gun control, and I wait for a knock on the companionway.

Sour-Drinks Set

At 4:00 a.m., you can't change anything, can't change that she's gone, that he moved to Miami. That early, you can't go anywhere, can't escape. If it weren't so cold downstairs, you could slip out of the covers and mix a margarita, but you don't have any Cointreau, so it'd taste sour anyway.

She did it at a nice place down by the theater district, slicing into her steak and then handing her rings across the table to him. Perhaps she thought undercooked forty-dollar meat would somehow make it easier. He went home and booked a trip to Cancun. Left the next day. Perhaps he thought buffets of overcooked meat and watered-down piña coladas would make it easier. But the piña coladas tasted sour. Maybe he should have tried the daiquiris.

Had the milk not gone sour that day, she wouldn't have gone to the store like that. And if she hadn't gone to the store like that, she wouldn't have been in the checkout line, wouldn't have commented on the flavor of ice cream he placed on the checkout conveyor belt (she noticed the ice cream only after noticing his blue eyes), wouldn't have said yes when he asked if she might want to get a coffee sometime. And so she wouldn't have been standing in front of this judge now, looking at a judgment sourer than the milk all those years ago.

So Happy

*S*he's happy, I think. *Look at her. That's happiness. She's pretty and thin, and she probably paid more than a hundred bucks for those highlights. I bet she doesn't have $10,487 in credit-card debt.*

I check for a ring. She has one—with a big rock. Probably two carats. It's nestled between two probably-sapphires. It's pretty.

I wish I were her. Her man's handsome. He has dark, thick hair and looks Hispanic to me. I know I'm stereotyping, but I bet he dances. I bet he takes her to Latin clubs in Houston on Friday nights and they get all wild and hot and sweaty on the dance floor. She probably wears three-inch heels and rocks a miniskirt and makes everyone look at her while she does salsa.

People look at her now. She looks like a model. Her bikini did not come from Walmart. I wasn't here when they put up her sun umbrella, but I'll bet the guy dug the hole in the sand for its support leg. She's all reclined on a towel under the shade of it, and people are admiring her, wishing they were her. She makes the Galveston beach look good.

This girl is too glamorous to wait tables at Chuy's like I do. And I doubt she dropped out of an accounting program with $30k in student loans and nothing to show for two wasted years. She and Mr. Hotness didn't meet online. She doesn't know what it's like to scour match.com profiles and go on dates with jobless dudes who call themselves screenwriters and grope you half an hour into dinner. This girl met her man dancing, I'm sure of it. He proposed at some all-inclusive in the Dominican Republic or Cancun. They got married at a church downtown and her dad walked her down the aisle, shedding one or two sweet tears when he saw his baby girl with her true love. My mom threw my dad out of the house when I was eight. I don't know where he is, so I couldn't ask him to walk me down the aisle, even if I had a guy who wanted more than to crash at my apartment while he writes the next big Netflix hit. And I'm in no hurry to find the man who smacked my mom one night and banged her head into a wall and called me retarded before going out and wrecking the pickup my mom had just paid off.

***

That girl's happy, she thinks from beneath her flowered beach umbrella. *Look, she doesn't have a cheating husband. . . . He didn't come home the other night. He is cheating, right? I'm not overreacting?*

I bet that girl has a decent job. She doesn't cut sweaty hair and pay too much rent at the salon. She's probably a real-estate agent or an accountant. She looks like an accountant. If she had a cheating husband, she could afford to leave him.

The woman runs a hand through her highlights, glances across the sand and watches the younger woman, whose bathing suit isn't high end, but it fits her well. The younger woman probably has a lot of girlfriends and they probably go out on Friday nights for margaritas and to flirt with good-looking men who have careers and would like to have kids one day.

I'll bet that bitch has nice parents, the woman thinks. *I'll bet she went to UT Austin or A and M, and I'll bet her parents paid for it. I'll bet she's in grad school now, probably studying something useless like French literature, so she can pretend to be impressive at the parties she goes to with those friends she has. She probably went to Europe when she was in undergrad and fell in love with Paris, so now she wants to teach French to high-school kids once she's done with school . . . because she looks nice and she has those nice parents and all that niceness makes her want to be nice to kids, to make the world a better place.*

The woman under the umbrella rolls her eyes behind the sunglasses she bought with her credit card. She looks out at the cargo ships on the horizon.

I'll bet those ships are going somewhere exotic, she thinks.

***

A woman walks away from the tourist amusement-park pier, shoving her wait-staff apron in her bag. *Look at all these tourists, she thinks. They look so relaxed, so happy.* A gull standing on the seawall seems to smile.

H@ppiness

I buy a ticket every winter. . . . Get good deals on the discount-travel websites. I look at the pictures of beaches and of colored drinks, with fruit shoved on the rims of the glasses. I arrive, and I eat the fruit, lifting the slices off the edge of the glass, before I take a sip of my first drink. But I still can't find the happiness. It's in the pictures, but when I get here, the concierge doesn't tell me where to find it.

@@@

Ch@rges

Until the prosecutor started coming around, no one thought much of poor widowed Mrs. Damien's old, oddly-timed proclamations that her husband was so sweet she could just kill and eat him.

The Showgirls

Jeff and I grew up together, so I know when he's completely blotto. And he was completely blotto that night. Of course, I wouldn't have told him he was blotto. I would have said he was shitfaced. I only use blotto in my head. I heard it in a movie when I was a kid and I've kept it for nights like that one on the Vegas Strip: for nights when the bad seed in my head wants to mock my best friend. But regardless—blotto or shitfaced—Jeff was *that* that night. Perhaps I wasn't much better, but I thought I was. We'd watched TV with a bottle of Bombay Sapphire in the room after drinking by the pool, and then we'd been at a bar in the Luxor Casino for a while before we'd moved over to New York-New York. Jeff had rambled on a little about wanting to get laid, but he hadn't really been trying and hadn't really talked to any women, other than the old chick who waited on us at the pub in New York-New York.

His remarks as we walked up the Strip after leaving New York-New York started off on that theme: getting laid. But Jeff was too drunk to stay there long. And the Strip provided so many topics.

"Do you think these motherfuckers make any money doing this shit?" He raised an arm toward a dirty Hello Kitty who had two kids posing in front of her and a mother snapping a picture.

The mother dropped a couple bucks in a bucket at Hello Kitty's side.

"She just made something." I tilted my thumb toward the frayed, stained cartoon cat.

Just beyond Hello Kitty, a dark dude in a dirty red t-shirt advertising the "tightest girls in Nevada" flicked his colorful escort-service cards as we passed and called out to us in rough, accented English about "sweet women."

"Like that fool. Does anyone take those cards?" Jeff asked.

"Someone must or they wouldn't be out here."

"I don't know." Jeff's head took in the Strip before us in a big, lazy, drunken arc. "I think it's all a scam," he said. "Fuckin' scam." Then he turned to me. "Life's a fuckin' scam, brother."

"Yep." I wasn't going to argue with him. We weren't to that point in the night. We were at the complacent point, the easy-going point, or at least, that's where I was.

Next after the escort hawker came the skanky "cops." One made eye contact.

"Come on, baby. You want a picture." The woman actually licked her lips at me.

"Yep, picture's fine," Jeff called, "but we'll skip the herpes, thanks."

As we'd been drinking at the casinos, the sun had set, and then it had gotten neon pseudo-dark, and then it had gotten quite late. Not late by Vegas standards, but late by the standard that had crept up on me unheard as I'd become an ostensible adult. The standard that put me in bed at ten each night and saw me rise at five to settle into a mild, nondescript sedan to make my mild, nondescript way to one of Houston's nondescript, if not mild, chemical companies. The standard that meant I had good health insurance, and a fluffy retirement account, and the means to buy Jeff a ticket to Vegas when his girlfriend Anita dumped him after two years. An odd standard that still didn't fit but which came in handy when Jeff and I wanted to spend money on booze and a show that had a stage full of women sliding around in a giant glass of water.

So as we walked down the Strip, I considered it late, even if Hello Kitty and the skanky cop, and Jeff, didn't. Jeff still tended bar at a trendy pub in the Woodlands, where he'd worked for years while telling everyone he was saving for law school. He hadn't yet slipped into the pool of insidious "maturity" in which I treaded water.

When the furred-handcuff-wielding cop yelled "fuck you" at Jeff's back, Jeff gave her the finger, and I frowned the way I thought people with retirement accounts should frown at flipping other people off like that.

"Come on, man," I said. "They're just trying to make a living."

"No, fuck that. They're on the make. Bunch of con artists. And those," he gestured over his shoulder, "are old-fashioned confidence whores." He snorted.

For lack of something better, I shrugged.

In front of me, Darth Vader fist bumped a kid who looked about ten. For a fleeting moment, I wondered about these kids—or their parents—out on the Strip this late. The kid's dad stopped and set the kid up beside the Sith lord and fiddled with his phone. Jeff walked between the dad and his subjects, ignoring that dad's efforts to freeze some sort of family memory. The neon overhead gyrated, teal and red and a color probably called goldenrod.

A man at my elbow inquired if we wanted discount tickets to a club for the evening. We ignored him, ignored the entrance to the Paris Casino, ignored the bad hip hop acoustically spraying us and the Strip's other pedestrians.

Two showgirls cooed at us, sporting pink feathers and rhinestone pasties.

"It'd be okay if I *wanted* to see that," Jeff said, "but those are some sloppy tits."

I looked over my shoulder and then agreed.

"Anita had great tits," Jeff said. It took him a breath or two to add, "Too bad she was a total bitch."

"It's okay, man." I put a hand on his shoulder. We'd met in third grade at Brookwood Elementary School on the southeast side of Houston when my dad relocated my family to Texas to take a job with NASA. Even back then, Jeff drank out of half-empty glasses.

"You know, she was fucking a dude in her Krav Maga class."

"Anita was doing Krav Maga?" I couldn't picture the HR admin with the ugly flats going all Shin Bet on someone's ass.

Jeff nodded, his eyes on the gum-pocked sidewalk.

Two characters from a Pixar movie I couldn't name leaned against a wall. One turned his back and removed his plastic helmet, scratched the birthmark on his cheek. We stopped at a storefront and bought tall, plastic, souvenir cups of something frozen and not alcoholic enough, the kind of drinks I generally associate with douche bags. Jeff sucked on his straw, a slurping hero, and then returned to his attack on the buskers.

"Piss off," he said to a woman who held out a pink-lighted toy she'd been shooting into the air and retrieving as it had parachuted back to earth.

The woman withdrew her toy, but rather than proffer it to the people coming along on our heels, as I expected her to do, she faced Jeff.

"Piss off yourself, buddy," she said.

"Sorry. My brother's drunk," I said to her.

She sniffed.

"It's hard enough standing out here selling these things without having assholes like him fuck with me."

Now I did feel bad. "Sorry," I repeated.

I put the plastic souvenir cup in my left hand and fumbled in my back pocket with my right, feeling slow and imprecise since the hours of drinking had overtaken my dexterity.

"Here," I said, holding out a fiver. "I'll take one."

The woman took the bill and dropped the perky pink light into my free hand.

"What the fuck was that?" Jeff asked as I caught up to him.

"Dude, she's just trying to make a living. No different than you hustling bachelorettes and old broads at the bar for tips."

"Yeah, whatever," Jeff said. "I've got a job. I work for a living. I'm not scamming people on the street."

"They're not scamming people. They're just offering services that are," I paused, "less conventional."

"They're offering bullshit to suckers." Jeff grabbed the pink toy from me and shot it up into the thick, starless sky, letting it fall to the sidewalk behind us as we kept walking.

"How do you know?" It must have been the frozen drink that kept me talking. "She probably got knocked up when she was sixteen and is just trying to put food on the table for her little bastard."

"Yeah, sure. That's it."

Two showgirls—this time in pale-blue feathers and high, platform boots—came into view, breasts sparkling in the lights of one of the older casinos, one with a pink-and-purple facade.

"Let's ask these chicks," I challenged, holding my plastic cup out toward the two women.

"What the fuck?" Jeff tilted his head when he turned to me.

"We'll just talk to them. Twenty bucks says they are normal chicks trying to make a living. Maybe going to school or some shit, but just, you know, trying to get by. And another twenty bucks says I can talk to 'em so they don't hit us up for money."

"Are you serious? Dude, you're going to lose. Those bitches are going to cry for money."

When we came abreast of the women, I stopped. They looked mid-twenties, and their pasties adorned finer racks than those of their sisters we had passed earlier.

"Hey, there." Both women were brunette, but the one who greeted us had lighter highlights.

"Hey," I said, "nice night to be in Vegas."

"Real nice night," Ms. Highlights said. "Where you from?"

"Houston," I answered. "Lone-star state."

"Ooh," the non-highlighted one piped up. "We like cowboys."

"Yeah, that's not us," I said. "We're in oil."

"For real?" Ms. Highlights adjusted a pasty without looking down at it. I couldn't tell if the gesture was intentional or subconscious.

"Yeah," I lied, "I'm a VP with Exxon. My brother's with Shell."

"Wow."

I'm not sure which one said it. For some reason, I'd shut my eyes to take a sip of my drink. When I opened my eyes, it took me a minute to right the sidewalk, which had started listing.

"So what do you ladies do?" I looked from the highlights to the other one, who had better legs. "Is this your full-time gig?"

"No," said Highlights. The tits supporting the mirrored pasties seemed to relax. "We just do this on our days off. We're in the cast at Tropics, and I'm at CSN. Um, the College of Southern Nevada."

"The cast?" I asked at the same time Jeff snorted and said, "Sure, what are you studying?"

"The cast at Tropics," Nicer Legs said to me, "is the elite group of service specialists who work the large functions for the Tropics Resort. Pool parties with celebrity guests, holiday extravaganzas, that kind of thing. We've met—" and she named two names that I associated with Hollywood but couldn't place beyond that.

While Legs addressed me, Highlights smiled at Jeff. "I'm studying cardiorespiratory sciences," she said. "Next June, I'll have my associates."

"Huh," I said. "What do you want to do?"

"I want to be a cardiac technician."

Her teeth, which betrayed her parents' inability to pay for braces, told me this career path would be a major accomplishment for her.

Jeff closed his lips over his straw and swirled the straw around his cup as he drank.

"You from Vegas originally?" I asked, not really focusing on one or the other of the girls.

"I'm from Cali," Highlights said.

"I'm from Michigan," Legs said.

"What towns?" I asked, not caring about the answers because I'd never been to Michigan and didn't know the state at all, and as far as

California was concerned, for me, it didn't extend beyond L.A., San Francisco, and maybe San Diego.

"Tulare," Highlights said in a way that sounded more like a question.

I nodded, sucking on my straw again.

"It's in the Central Valley, south of Fresno," she said, this time making it sound like an apology. "It's a big agricultural area. Lot of dairy."

"I'm from Battle Creek," Legs said. "It's like here." She held up a hand in the shape of a mitten and pointed at the fleshy part way below the pinky. "It's where Kellogg's Cereal is based out of. Boring as fuck. That's why I came out here."

"But you're just working out here?" I asked. "Not doing the school thing, too?"

"Nope," she said. "I work a lot. I send money home to my mom. She's on disability. She's diabetic and has a lot of problems because of it. She's legally blind and has a lot of nerve issues. Like in her feet. She can't get around real well."

"Aw, that's a bummer."

"Yeah, well." She shrugged. "She rides one of those Amigos."

"So what do you girls do for fun?" Jeff asked. "Like what clubs do you like?"

"Oh, well," Highlights laughed a little, "that stuff is all work for us. We don't really go out when we've got time off. We, uh, we read and Keera likes photography."

"Oh, wow," I said. "That's cool." My right hand was cold and wet from the chill and condensation of my tall cup. I switched the cup to my left hand and wiped my right on my jeans and then put it on the back of my neck for a minute.

"Yeah," Highlights continued, "she's really good at it. We have amazing pictures in our apartment."

"What do you like to read?" Jeff asked neither girl specifically.

"Which artists do you admire?" I asked Legs—or Keera.

"Um, I really like Ansel Adams," Legs/Keera replied as Highlights said, "I'm a hopeless romantic."

Highlights giggled. "I love romance novels. Love to think Prince Charming could just come by and sweep me away." She waved a hand through the pink and purple light around us. Then she giggled again, making the rhinestones dangling from her nipples shake.

"So what's your favorite book?" Jeff sounded smug to me, but I'm not sure the girls caught the tone.

"Um, uh." Highlights tapped her chin and stared upward, feathered headdress tilting back. "Um, you know, I'm going to say *The Iliad*. It's not a romance, but it's a classic. For romances, I'd say *Pride and Prejudice*."

Jeff raised an eyebrow at me. I hoped the smile I offered in reply looked self-satisfied.

"So how long do you stay out here?" Jeff asked. "Like when you're hustling, like tonight."

"Oh, it depends," Legs/Keera answered. "Depends on whether people are tipping well, how tired we get, you know."

"How tired are you now?" Jeff asked.

"Well, that depends too," Legs/Keera replied. She bent down and messed with her boot, but she did it at an angle, presenting her fishnet-covered ass. "My feet kinda hurt," she said, straightening up. "That boot's been bugging me all night."

A video screen up the Strip projected a new scene, changing the mix of the glow around us, and I noticed Jeff move his attention from Keera's ass back to his now-empty drink.

"Well," he said, and I saw his eyes flicker, "my brother and I could buy you a couple drinks to dull the pain. Um, from your boot hurting."

Highlights looked at Keera. Jeff looked at me in that instant of psychological privacy. I grinned, and I'm sure I looked pretty drunk when I did it.

"Okay," Highlights said a moment later. "Keera knows a guy who owns a bar near our place. We can drink pretty cheap there."

"Especially if we don't change." Keera laughed and reached beneath her breasts and jiggled them a little.

"How, um, how far is it?" I asked. "I can get us an Uber."

The girls exchanged glances again.

"Sure," Keera said, "that'd be nice. But you don't have to, or we can give you money for it."

I shot another victory glance at Jeff.

"No way," I said, "I got this."

"Okay," Keera said, and she picked up the girls' tip bucket and began to lead the way toward the Uber pick-up area of the old-school pink-and-purple casino.

"You want me to carry that?" Jeff asked.

"Aw, I got it, honey," Keera replied.

The Uber driver introduced himself as Tally and asked if we were comfortable in his Nissan Sentra. Jeff said we were fine and thanked him for stopping. In the back seat, Keera sat between me and Highlights and I listened to the two women chatter about the schedule at Tropics until Keera called Highlights 'Manda, and then I tuned out. All I'd needed was a name.

"Here we go," Tally announced when he stopped the Nissan outside a dark stucco building with a flashing red sign.

As I fumbled with the door handle, my drunkenness relented just enough to let me feel a little wary about going into the club with these women. The fishnet coverings and blue feathers over the women's asses, however, blew the feeling aside as the fishnet stretched tighter with the women's efforts to crawl out of the Sentra. The bouncer at the entrance greeted the women by name. He gestured at Jeff's and my plastic cups and then at a trashcan near the door. After we'd dumped the cups, he told us to pay the cover charge inside. I forked over forty bucks for me, Jeff, and the two showgirls to get Tyvek wristbands.

"What would you like to drink?" Jeff shouted over the throb of house music.

Both women asked for cosmos. Jeff shrugged, mumbled "Guinness" to me, and followed the blue feathers to a booth as I went toward the bar. When I brought the drinks to the table a few minutes later, Amanda was telling Jeff she had a thing for Andy Warhol paintings. Keera said she loved Marilyn Monroe and that Marilyn's image had helped inspire her to be a showgirl. Jeff asked Keera about her photography, and Keera giggled and took a long sip of vodka and triple sec.

"I gotta pee," she shouted as she put the drink down. "I'll be right back."

"I gotta pee, too," Amanda yelled. She followed her friend to the back of the club.

"What the fuck are we doing," I yelled at Jeff.

"Proving you right," he shouted back. "They're fine. And they've got nice asses."

We sat back in our chairs, beneath the four-four pulse and synthesized basslines. The girls stayed away a long time, and I had a vague thought about whether they might be snorting cocaine in the back. But they returned to the table finally and sat down and seemed fine. Jeff asked something about Keera's sick mom and Keera said something about insulin and alcohol pads and then something about prescription plans. I couldn't hear her well and I didn't care. Jeff got up and then returned with two more cosmos and a gin and tonic for himself. I was too drunk to feel annoyed that I had to get up and go to the bar for my own Negroni. Or that Jeff asked me to get him one too, the bastard.

In the Uber to the women's apartment many, many drinks later, Jeff sat in the front seat and I sat in the back with the showgirls. Jeff twisted around and patted Keera's knee.

"Your mom is lucky to have a daughter like you," he crooned.

"Sure, sure," I shouted. "Both your moms are real lucky."

"Here," Jeff said, squirming in the front seat to pull his wallet out of a pocket. "Here." He handed a Benjamin back to Keera. "Here, send her that when you send stuff to her next time."

"Aw, you don't have to." Keera took the bill, but let it hang in her fingers in the space over the car's center console.

"No, no, I want to. You're a good person to do what you do." Jeff turned back to face the windshield.

When we made it up the stairs to the apartment and stumbled inside, I was struggling to see things clearly. Still, drunkenness aside, I'm pretty sure there were no artistic photographs or Andy Warhol posters displayed on the living-room walls. But I'm also sure I was feeling anything but mild and nondescript.

*

They call it a gentlemen's club, but the only men
I've met at work are pigs.

7 Down: Bachata

Across from her on the subway, a dude about Rachel's age sat with what appeared to be a book of crossword puzzles. He raised his head, caught her looking, smiled under shaggy, surfer-boy hair that fell in his eyes.

"What's a popular genre of Latin music that originated in the Dominican Republic in the 1960s and was originally associated with houses of ill repute?"

Rachel blinked. Was he asking her?

No one else sat nearby.

She bit her lip, grinned. "*Bachata.* B-A-C-H-A-T-A."

The guy cocked his head, held her eyes. Then he checked his newsprint book. "Yep, that fits perfectly." He paused. "And hey, that makes this one across 'heretic,' so that works." He looked up. "Thanks."

The subway car warmed up. Rachel rubbed the top of her gray backpack with a fingertip.

"How'd you know that?" he asked.

"I like to dance," she answered. "I do ballroom and swing and stuff, but Latin club dances are my favorite: salsa, *bachata*, cha cha cha, merengue, *kizomba*, *zouk*. That kind of thing."

"Wow." The dude leaned across the aisle. "I'm Jake." He held out his hand.

"Rachel," she replied. She tried to think of a follow-up question, but her shyness swamped her efforts.

"So do you listen to a lot of *bachata* music?" Jake kept leaning toward her, as much as the jerking of the car would allow.

"I do," she said. "I like the mainstream stuff. Romeo Santos, Prince Royce, Enrique Iglesias, but what I really like is the hardcore stuff like Luis Vargas. Real Dominican stuff. It's pretty cool. You should try it sometime. It's like—" she fished through her head for the word. Couldn't quite find it. "It's like the ultimate pickmeup. It frees you. It's like this magic spell to make you happy and confident and," she didn't catch herself in time, couldn't stop herself, "beautiful." The blush rushed up her neck.

Darn it.

"Do you ever teach people? Like teach them to dance?"

***

When they got married two years later, they performed a *bachata* as their first dance. They honeymooned in Punta Cana and spent every night dancing to merengue and *bachata* and drinking piña coladas. Their oldest daughter Lydia won the Junior Five-Dance International Latin competition at Ohio Star Ball when she was six years old. And Jake knew it was all his fault when everything unraveled.

Because by taking his secretary Diane to Punta Cana for a tryst, all those years later, by teaching Diane what *bachata* was and dancing with her, he broke the spell. He broke it all.

Cumbia

The dancefloor expanded, the *cumbia* rhythm wrapping us into a womb of heartbeats and hips. I held her against me and knew elation and despair, for she would stay until she wouldn't, and I would be left broken, with only a memory of how big one song could grow.

*

She begged me for another chance. Suggested we spend a day at the Met. Just the two of us. Get ice cream afterward . . . and talk. We'd talk. Now I'm standing alone in front of a Greek sarcophagus. Her text said she had to "work."

She didn't bother with an .

True India

Roy Arden didn't know that together his parents brought $340,000.00 a year home to the family's traditional brick bi-level with the detached garage and five bedrooms. Roy knew he got the video games and clothes and phones and tablets he asked for for Christmas, but he didn't keep tabs on the numbers, of course. And he had only a vague idea that his parents brought home bonuses each winter, after the year-end books closed at BASF and LyondellBasell.

Kids like Roy don't understand the details of such things. They don't know that, if the companies to which their parents drive each morning rearrange and recombine enough molecules all year, their parents will get extra money—sometimes a lot of extra money. Of course, kids like Roy don't understand the intricacies of molecules and chemicals and making America happy with the things chemicals make: plastic things and synthetic things and cutting-edge things. Kids understand being happy, or they think they do, but they don't understand the details. Roy didn't know that each Christmas his parents vowed the coming bonuses would go toward paying down the family's healthy five-figure credit-card debt. And he didn't know his parents broke these vows each spring.

Instead of going toward the debt, the bonuses went to things like paying for the tennis tournaments that Roy Arden won to become a Super-Champ-division player in Texas junior tennis. Roy, of course, knew about the tournaments. He knew about the weekly lessons he took to make him the top player on Pine Lake High School's varsity tennis team.

He also knew, in a vague way, that his parents' bonuses paid to feed the family, though again, he didn't keep tabs on the numbers or distinguish between salaries and bonuses. He knew his dad loved the duck at Ibiza in midtown, with the Brussels-sprout leaves and natural pan jus. He himself favored the crab-stuffed shrimp at Gaido's, on the island, with the family sharing the aptly described family-sized sides of au gratin potatoes or blue-cheese grits. He knew his mother protested but then got a peach bellini or two when they went to Gaido's. And he knew how happy his parents sounded when they loaded him—Roy— back in the pewter-colored BMW X5 M and Mr. Arden drove them all away from the seawall after such a meal.

Roy knew how, on Sundays, his mother would suggest they "get adventurous" and go to the brunch buffet at Mogul's or True India. He would watch his parents pile their plates high with chicken tikka masala and garlic naan. He himself would dig into the chicken vindaloo. Maybe True India was a little unprepossessing, snuggled as it was in the strip mall between the pho place and the Bike Barn, but it did have the best pakoras.

Things his parents' bonuses did not pay for included the high-school tennis team's raffle tickets. And Roy knew this. In the fall of his sophomore year, he brought home the book of raffle tickets—worth a total of $125. The coaches gave each player a book to sell. As far as Roy knew, most team parents were going to purchase the tickets rather than sit at a card table in front of the HEB or Kroger or Randalls for a couple still-quite-hot fall Sunday afternoons. They would buy the tickets themselves instead of hawking the things to other parents in the top 5% of American earners. The Ardens, however, did not see themselves that way: as parents who would just buy the tickets rather than give their son a chance to learn marketing and business skills by letting him peddle the tickets on his own. But neither did they see themselves sitting at a folding table on the curb in front of the supermarket.

Instead, Mrs. Arden suggested Roy talk to his coaches and develop a sales strategy for unloading the tickets. So one afternoon, Roy approached the assistant tennis coach after practice. Coach Griffin looked down at the boy, whose five-foot-four frame belied the power of the teen's serve.

"Your parents won't take you to the HEB? The managers over there are always really good to us. They'll set up a table for you and you can sell the tickets on weekends. They'll be gone in a weekend if you stay out there awhile. See if you can get a teammate to go with you. You can both sell your tickets that way."

Roy shifted, dug an Adidas Barricade toe into the concrete of the parking lot.

Coach Griffin tried to judge the boy's reaction.

"Well," the coach decided to continue, "Olivia sold all her tickets by asking the managers at Gordon's and P.J. Farley's to buy the tickets and give them to patrons as a little bonus and thank you. The servers put the tickets in the bill folders—you know . . . the folder thing the receipt comes in? Well, the waitresses are putting the tickets in those folders for the customers. The customers can check Facebook and see if they've won next month after the raffle."

Coach Griffin looked at his watch.

"Try that, buddy. Where do your folks eat? Go in there and see if the manager will buy the tickets. But I gotta go now. My wife's got a thing tonight, so I'm going to P.J. Farley's myself to watch the game."

"Okay, Coach. Thanks," Roy said. He hefted his Babolat bag over a shoulder and turned toward the front of the school where he would catch a ride home with an older teammate.

After service that Sunday, Mrs. Arden asked her husband and son where they wanted to go for brunch. Roy contemplated suggesting Gordon's, with its manger's largesse toward rising tennis stars, but he knew his mother's thoughts about the self-styled "brewhouse," and he didn't want to explain Coach Griffin's plan for unloading the tickets. Trying to explain could lead to worse options, like a suggestion to go door-to-door in the neighborhood.

"I'm feeling tandoori chicken," Mr. Arden said, his eyes seeking his son's in the BWM's rearview mirror. "How about you, Mr. Roy?"

Roy tapped through the Imgur memes and videos flowing across the iPhone X's screen. "Sure." His head didn't rise from the drama unfolding before him as a middle-aged man misjudged his ability to effect a trampoline stunt.

"Honey?" Mr. Arden lowered his eyes from the mirror and rested them on his wife.

"Sure, bae." Mrs. Arden grinned.

In the seat behind her, her son cringed the silent cringe of suffering youth.

"How about the True India buffet?" Again, the father's eyes in the mirror.

Roy shrugged, the eyes on him unseen.

"Sure, honey," Mrs. Arden said. She pulled her X out of her Kate Spade.

Mr. Arden turned onto Bayfront Boulevard.

In the parking lot of the margarine-colored stucco strip mall, Mr. Arden slipped the BMW into a spot facing True India and hustled out his door and around the SUV to open his wife's door. Roy put his phone in the back pocket of his Tom Fords and followed his parents through the glass door into the modest little dining room with its scarred booths and the crane mural that confessed the place's previous life as Hunan Palace. True India's round, chestnut-colored proprietor hurried over to the Ardens, smiling and then shaking Mr. Arden's hand.

"Welcome back, sir," Mr. Sengupta said.

"We need our tandoori-chicken fix, Mr. Sengupta," Mr. Arden replied.

The family slid into a booth and Mr. Sengupta returned with a water pitcher. When he'd finished with the Ardens' water glasses, he bustled over to the only other customers in the small space, a young couple who appeared to be of Indian descent.

"Shall we hit the feed trough?" Mr. Arden slid out of the booth and led the way to the chrome-and-curry-colored buffet.

Three platefuls later, Mrs. Arden declared herself full and set her paper napkin beside her plate.

"Everything was all right?" Mr. Sengupta appeared beside the Ardens' booth.

"Delicious," Mrs. Arden confirmed.

"Too good," Mr. Arden said, patting his belly.

"How is school for you?" Mr. Sengupta looked at Roy. "You are at Pine Lake?"

"Yeah, Pine Lake. It's fine," Roy said.

"You like it?"

"Nah. It's mostly boring."

"Oh, you say that now, but you'll see later. You need to study and get good grades to go to a good college, eh?" Mr. Sengupta gathered up plates and the empty naan basket.

"Maybe." Roy put his elbow on the table and his head in his hand.

"I will bring your check over." Mr. Sengupta nodded at Mr. Arden.

"Hey," Roy pushed himself back from the table, "can I ask if they'll buy my raffle tickets here to give to customers? Coach Griffin said Olivia Harvey sold all her tickets at Gordon's and P.J. Farley's. I guess the managers bought them to give to people as a bonus with their checks."

Mrs. Arden had her compact open. She rubbed the tube of Dolce and Gabbana royal pink over her pout and then snapped the mirror closed.

"Honey?" She looked at her husband.

Mr. Arden glanced around the almost empty room.

"I don't know if this is really a tennis-raffle place, Mr. Roy," he said.

Roy shrugged. "I just thought I could try."

Mr. Arden glanced at his wife and then over his shoulder toward the cash register and the counter where the staff handled take-out orders.

"Well, I suppose you can ask," he said. "Can't hurt to ask. If they aren't up for it, they'll just say no. And they know us. We're in here all the time. Sure, go ahead and ask, but if they say no, just thank them, okay?"

"I know, Dad."

When Mr. Sengupta returned with the check, Roy set his phone down.

"Mr. Sengupta?"

"Yes?"

"I'm on the tennis team at Pine Lake and I just thought I'd ask you something. We're selling raffle tickets as a team fundraiser. They're five bucks a piece and the prizes include massages at Zen Solutions, a hundred-dollar gift card at Jocelyn's Custom Jewelry, movie passes at the Cinema 12, and some other stuff I can't remember. A bunch of places donated prizes."

Mr. Sengupta stood attentive beside the table, his smile unwavering.

"Um," Roy continued, "a couple places bought ticket books to give their patrons tickets at the end of their meals. Um, Gordon's and P.J. Farley's. The waiters give the tickets to people with their bills and then people can log in next month and see if they won anything. It's only $125 for a book of twenty-five tickets. I've got a book in the car."

Mr. Arden saw Mr. Sengupta's eyes flicker.

"No need to buy them if they won't help your business, Mr. Sengupta," he said. "No need at all. Roy's just learning to be a little salesman."

The proprietor shifted.

"Oh, no. It's fine. Yes, I'll buy your tickets." He nodded at Roy and handed the family's check to Mr. Arden. "I'll go get money from the register."

Roy slid out of the booth.

"Here, Dad, lemme have the keys. I'll go get the tickets."

While Roy went to the car, Mr. Arden gave Mr. Sengupta a Visa for the $41.28 tab and left an eight-dollar tip.

When Roy returned with the ticket book, Mr. Sengupta counted fifty-five ones, eight fives, and three ten-dollar bills into Roy's hand.

"One hundred twenty-five," he said. "Thank you." He took the ticket book from the teenager.

"Thank you, Mr. Sengupta," Roy replied.

The Ardens thanked Mr. Sengupta and the woman who came out of the kitchen to wave, and the threesome headed out into the Texas warmth.

"Well, that was nice, wasn't it?" Mrs. Arden shifted her purse to her other arm, so she could take her husband's hand. "Look at that, Mr. Roy. You sold all your tickets. Good for you."

"Where to now?" Mr. Arden asked as he opened Mrs. Arden's door to the SUV. "Anybody want froyo?"

"Sure!" Mrs. Arden said.

Roy snorted at a meme and his father accepted that as a "yes."

A few hours later, when Mrs. Arden decided to take the family's tea-cup Pomeranian Leeann for a walk, she realized she'd misplaced her sunglasses.

"Honey," she called up the stairs, "honey, have you seen my sunglasses?"

Mr. Arden sat before his NFL Sunday Ticket and couldn't remember the last time he'd noticed his wife in her sunglasses.

"No, honey," he shouted.

"Honey," Mrs. Arden called up again, "I must have left them at the Indian place. I guess I'll have to drive over there. I can't go without my sunglasses."

Mr. Arden sighed. "I'll go over there with you."

He pushed the old footrest of the recliner down and lumbered out of the chair. As tatty as the thing was, he couldn't bear to part with it.

"I wouldn't care so much, but I can't drive without them tomorrow," Mrs. Arden continued shouting. "And I hate to lose them. They're my Guccis. Some little Indian girl probably has them now and I won't get them back. Oh, well. It's my fault for not being careful. But let's see if we can get them back. I hate to lose them."

Upstairs, Mr. Arden slipped his feet into his Birkenstocks and followed his wife's voice to the stairway.

"Come on, honey, let's go find your glasses," he called as he descended.

In the kitchen, he picked up his keys from the leather valet bowl he'd bought in Cozumel that past January. Then he looked at his Submariner.

"We should shake a leg," he said to his wife. "They close at three on Sundays. They only do that brunch buffet."

"Oh," Mrs. Arden said, "we aren't going to make it. Never mind. I'll worry about it this week."

"No, honey, come on." Mr. Arden took her arm. "We've got what? Eight minutes? We'll make it. And it's not like they're going to lock the door right at three. People will still be eating, you know? Wrapping up. Let's go."

The couple walked out to the driveway and got in the SUV. Mr. Arden backed down the drive and turned toward the neighborhood's gateway and Bayfront Boulevard. At the Bike Barn strip mall, he made a left and pulled in and nosed the vehicle into a spot in front of the little Indian eatery's storefront.

"Here we go, honey. You want me to go in with you?"

"No, sweetie, I'll just hop out and go get them." Mrs. Arden slid out of the vehicle and stepped toward the restaurant's glass door.

Someone had already darkened the "open" sign, and the lights inside the space appeared to be off. The place radiated a feeling of slumber, but the door opened when Mrs. Arden pulled. She stepped in and there stood Mr. Sengupta, his round back to her, his shirt stained beneath the arms and around the collar. He was unwrapping his apron from around himself. In the booths lay three adults and a girl who looked about ten. An elderly lady who could have been Mrs. Arden's mother's age was removing a bright red-and-gold embroidered cloth from around her shoulders. She smoothed it over the seat of another booth and lay down on it, seeming not to notice Mrs. Arden.

"Oh, madam," Mr. Sengupta said. He ran a hand through his hair and his eyes darted around the room where his family was trying to sleep. "I'm sorry. We're closed now. If you'd like something to go, I'll—"

"Oh, no, no." Mrs. Arden touched his arm. "Oh, no, I'm sorry. I just, I just wanted to see if I'd left my sunglasses here. Some Gucci sunglasses. Big— big lenses," she faltered. "Red on top."

"Oh, no, I'm sorry, madam. No one has seen anything like that. They would have put them in the drawer under the cash register, but we found no sunglasses today."

The little girl stirred, made a kitten-like sound and rolled over.

"I'm— I'm sorry to have bothered you. Thank you." Mrs. Arden backed away, pushing the door open against her shoulder blades and retreating out into the autumn-afternoon sun. "Have a good evening."

She turned and walked back to the silver BMW.

"Any luck?" Mr. Arden turned John Mayer down as his wife climbed into the car.

"No. No one turned anything in."

On the hop home, Mrs. Arden found her glasses in the cubby beneath the arm rest.

Stuffing Set

"I— I can't." Her voice cracked, faltered.

(A crash behind him, a wrong-sounding mix of skateboard wheels on park concrete . . . and a sticky organic cracking. He didn't turn to look, to see the wreck. He just kept looking at her and she just kept looking at the pavement, or he thought she was looking at the pavement. It looked that way to him.)

"Someone got the stuffing knocked out of them," she finally whispered. She still wouldn't look at him, and he still couldn't look anywhere but at her. So he saw her looking over his shoulder at whatever lay behind him, at whomever had made the terrible sound of hurt and blood and speed ending all at once on concrete.

And she was right about that, about the stuffing getting knocked out of someone, regardless of whatever had happened behind him. Finally, he glanced away and got up off his knee and re-boxed the glittering ring.

After she kicked the stuffing out of him, he emptied his bank account and bought a ticket to Tahiti. On the island, he got most of himself stuffed all back inside. Learned to dive. Saw dolphins. Now he sits on the beach at night and tells himself he doesn't remember her.

Some people lose their families to fiery car crashes. Or earthquakes or shark attacks, I think. To cancers and ill fate and things you don't have to blame them for. I lost mine slowly, piece by piece, drop by drop, year by year. To angry text messages and secret credit cards and "that time when. . . ." The stuffing just seeping out. I don't know if blaming would make it easier.

Beneath the spray of blue and red lights, it wasn't the blood or pieces of bumper or the severed and bent wheel lying on the highway's shoulder—but rather the crumpled pink box with its wedding-cake stuffing oozing out—that made Patrick's stomach twist as he loaded the woman into the ambulance.

"Something Missing"
(part of *Stuffing*)

It was way past too-late, but she kept at it: kept stuffing missing-person fliers into mailboxes, kept kneeling at the foot of the bed, kept calling on St. Michael. And (secretly, not on purpose) kept hoping he *had* taken Jenny . . . that he *was* all bad . . . that it *wasn't* just Jenny's choice.

When she got like that (the crying and the shaking), he'd climb out of bed, turn on the hallway light, digging his old Martin out of the closet, stuffing between its strings every happy memory he could find in the songs she loved. And when she finally smiled, he remembered the happy too.

Dispute

Something shook the kink out of the hose and the words sprayed out, soaking me and Brett and the kilim wall hangings we got at the Grand Bazaar in Istanbul on our honeymoon. We had hung the pretty, rough textiles as soon as we'd gotten home from the trip, warming up the condo with pinks and purples and golds. After we'd hung them all, Brett had put in a Tarkan CD we'd bought over there, and we'd danced awkwardly on the kitchen's bamboo flooring, having forgotten everything we'd learned in our wedding-dance classes. Those classes wouldn't have helped us with Tarkan anyway, but we still mentioned them that night we hung the kilims, and we laughed over how we'd forgotten everything the minute we'd finished that bridal rhumba in front of my mom and his parents and my sorority sisters.

That all happened long ago, though—the dancing in the kitchen and hanging up the textiles, and my sorority sisters watching me rhumba in a white dress with a bustle. All that happened long before I drenched us—drenched Brett and the kilims—in this wet, sticky mess of

"I don't respect you."

The mess now drips off everything. It drips off the walls and my fingertips and Brett's chin. It puddles around our feet and soaks into our socks, and it is starting to produce a weird smell.

Brett doesn't say anything. He doesn't move. I know he is breathing, that he can smell whatever it is I am smelling. But I only know that because he's standing in front of me and we've lived together for eight years and I know Brett has really sensitive olfactories. It's not because he moves or gestures or even blinks. No, he just stands there.

Brett's eyes look like the sparky little gold lights of the luminaries my dad used to put out in the yard when I was little. My dad grew up in New Mexico, so he would put these Spanish candle things in our yard in Ann Arbor, Michigan, every winter. It would start in early November. Dad would bring home these small paper bags and give them to me and my sister to punch holes in with these janky little chrome-plated hole punchers. The male and female parts of the punchers never quite lined up, so my sister and I had to wrestle with the things to get the holes punched, and the holes never came out quite round. They had these raggedy or distended shapes because we'd had to smash those hole-punching jaws down over and over to get the jaws to punch anything out.

My sister and I would draw angels and stars on the bags and try to punch holes all along the outlines and in decorative patterns inside the outlines, but the patterns wouldn't come out right and we'd be disappointed. Dad would tell us they looked great, but we knew the truth. We'd do a few bags each evening, and then, the night of Thanksgiving, it would happen. Dad would get out all the bags and flick them open and scoop handfuls of sand into them. The sand settled in their bottoms to weigh the bags down. He and my sister and I would then carry all the slightly-heavy bags outside, and Dad would line the things up along our Michigan driveway and the footpath to the front door and along the flowerbeds between the door and the garage. He'd give me and my sister votive candles and we would crouch over each bag and dig a small hole in the sand in the bag's bottom and put a votive in the indent and pat the sand around it with our kid fingers.

When we had finished all that, when the bags stood brown and papery with their frowzy, asymmetrical stars and seraphim, Dad would walk to the front door and open it just enough to put his head in. He'd shout for my mom to come out, and then the three of us would wait on the lawn. My mom would emerge and Dad would hand her the long barbeque lighter and say, "*Mi alma*, would you do the honors?"

My mom would sigh because she would be in her shirt sleeves. My sister and I never understood why she'd go outside in Michigan at the end of November without a coat, but our mom would do just that to light the luminaries. She'd shiver and fuss and question the wisdom of burning candles in paper bags, but she'd light them all. And then the four of us would stand in the driveway, and my dad's eyes would look brighter than the bags, and my sister and I would giggle and poke each other, and my mom would blow on her fingers and dwell on the cold and be the first one to go back inside.

Some people call luminaries *farolitos*. One could translate *farolito* as "little lighthouse" if one were an eleven-year-old girl whose dad had packed up the car and driven back to New Mexico after that one last, final fight with the girl's mom. I translated it that way for a few years—until high school. My sister and I kept punching holes in bags and dropping votive candles in sandy bottoms for a while. We thought, in the way silly little girls do, that maybe the lights might guide Dad home. But then we went to high school and got boyfriends and realized the way life works, the way men don't come back when you tell them you don't respect them.

*

I turned 21 that day. And we went out drinking that night. Even after seeing all that on TV: the buildings and the planes and the smoke (really dark, thick smoke) and the tiny black specks of people falling through blue space. Blue space and black smoke. I regret that . . . going out drinking. Even now. All these years later. I should have dug around for my mom's old rosary or something. I still don't know where that rosary is.

Spring Break

The day marked our six-month anniversary, so I surprised Jillian with dinner at Marko's. She loved the place and I liked the idea of candlelight. It was still too early, but I'll confess I'd been looking at jewelry. When work got slow. Looking for the kind of ring that makes a girl like Jillian say "yes." Jillian was the kind of girl who said yes to climbing in Yosemite and rafting down the Grand Canyon, but she'd never said yes to taking on a permanent dive buddy or kayaking partner, and I was hoping to change that.

"We should do something over spring break," I ventured, watching her swirl her wine in maroon waves around her glass.

"Sure," she said. "What are you thinking?"

I paused, trying to figure out a "good answer": should it be something adventurous (pure Jillian) or something comfortable, even luxurious (my default after twenty-five years of enjoying upstream oil money in Houston)?

"How about skiing?" The perfect combination. We would stay at a nice resort, a rustic fireplace and private soaking pool. I knew just the place north of Santa Fe. And Jillian could have her fun sliding down a mountain. I'd snowboarded enough to figure I wouldn't embarrass myself.

"Sure," Jillian said again, not waiting to consider. "Where do you want to go?"

I slid my bread through the bath of olive oil and herbs between us. "How about Santa Fe? We could make a little roadtrip of it. Drive out there, ski, stay someplace nice, have some nice meals. How does that sound?"

"I'm in." She sat back as the waitress placed her swordfish in front of her.

After Jillian fell asleep that night, I got online and booked two rooms at $519 each a night. Spring break meant no promo codes . . .

and two rooms because Jillian had agreed to taking Helmut with us, and Helmut's mom had agreed when I had texted her. I just hadn't talked to Helmut yet.

When we piled into the I-Pace a week later, Helmut didn't express any thirteen-year-old excitement or curiosity about his first ski trip. He pulled out a book with some sort of elf knight on the cover and hunkered down behind my seat, out of the path of the review mirror. Jillian made her standard remarks about doubting the environmental benefits of electric cars given the scourge of lithium batteries. I pulled onto I-45 and turned up Kid Rock.

We stopped in Fort Worth and I let Helmut talk me into an early lunch at a Cheesecake Factory. Jillian rolled her eyes and sat behind her own book, one adorned with a picture of a whitewater raft, as we waited for the hostess to seat us. In Amarillo, we pit-stopped at the Golden Arches and Jillian refused even a bottle of water (the scourge of plastic), and I let Helmut get cookies and a fountain drink to complement his cheeseburger. We ate inside the restaurant, rather than in the car, and I had the raft picture off the cover of Jillian's book memorized by the end of the "meal." By the state line, Helmut was sound asleep and Jillian had arranged a hot spot with her cell phone and was "working."

"Where are we?" my son asked when he woke up.

"Santa Rosa," I replied, glancing in the mirror to no avail. My boy lay across the seat in a pile of blue blanket and black backpack.

"How much farther?"

At least he'd taken an interest. "Less than two hours. We're close."

He didn't say anything else.

I patted Jillian's knee. She looked up from her laptop screen and smiled at me and then returned to her keyboard.

They stayed in the SUV when I went into the lodge to check us into the resort a couple hours later. The woman at the registration desk made positive remarks about the snow conditions and promised me that I and "my family" would have a great time on the slopes. Her enthusiasm, the thin, clear air, and the navy-colored, star-embroidered velvet cloak overhead outside reinvigorated me and made me believe the woman was right: we were going to have a great time.

In the room, Jillian ate both chocolates off the pillows from the turn-down service but declined a dip in our patio hot tub.

"You sure, honey? I'll bet it'd feel great after the drive." I stripped out of my jeans and hung them over the back of a chair.

"Looks like someone wants more than a soak in the tub." Jillian wrinkled her nose at me and pouted her lips, sly and flirty.

Thirty-two years old and wearing only a thong, she knew she was going to have that effect on me. I reached out, caught her, and stroked a thumb across a sweet pink nipple.

"Sweetheart, I'm beat." She pushed my hand away, peeled off her thong, and pulled the covers back from the bed. "You can go soak for a bit. You know, you should. You did all that driving. I'm going to hit the hay, though. We should get up fairly early to get a good start tomorrow."

Tomorrow did come early, with Jillian's phone chirping an alert at six-thirty. I rolled over and into her naked heat and slipped a hand between her thighs. She grunted and rolled away from me, pulling her phone off the nightstand.

"It's nothing," she mumbled. "Just Twitter." She set the phone back down beneath the bedside light.

"Well, I'll give you something that's not nothing." I cringed as soon as the words were out. Had I become such an "old man"? I tried to open her legs, but she squirmed away, giving me a light kiss and a pull on my cock that made me grind my teeth.

"Come on, sweetheart," she said, sliding out of the bed, "we should get going. It's going to be a good day."

She pranced past the foot of the bed, all smooth mounds of ass and tits and tiny waist, and into the bathroom. I deflated, falling back against the pillows and rubbing the paunch that had shown up one day when I hadn't been looking. Then I pulled my own phone away from its charger and tapped to call my son.

"What?" Helmut had never been easy to force into wakefulness.

"You ready to go snowboarding?" While the trip had started out more about me and Jillian, I did feel excited about taking my son on his first mountain adventure.

"No, I want to sleep, Dad. It's my spring break." He sighed.

I didn't know how to respond. I couldn't fault the kid. I wanted to sleep, too. And romance Jillian. And go in that hot tub. But I could hear the water running in the shower.

"Jillian's already in the shower, buddy. It's time to get up. If we get up now, we can have a nice breakfast in the lodge."

We could have had a nice breakfast in the lodge any time I wanted. But here we were, so up we would get.

Helmut made a sound of frustration.

"We'll knock on your door in half an hour." I ended the call and threw the covers back.

I was bent over my waterproof duffle, pulling out ski supplies when Jillian emerged—without a towel on. She leaned over me, strawberry nipples still warm and wet from the shower pressing into my back. She smelled like melon and something thick and musky.

"Okay, one quick one," she whispered, dropping to her knees and pulling my boxers down. I was in her mouth before I knew it, groaning, the long drive suddenly so worth it. She had me within her moments later, and I didn't last long. She showered a second time, rubbing soap on me with her body, and we still managed to make it to Helmut's door in forty minutes.

"You look mad sexy," she whispered as we walked to the lodge.

The breakfast was almost as good as the sex, and suddenly I felt like I was on vacation. We were in the ski center's parking lot forty-five minutes after throwing the bags in the back of the SUV, and Jillian fondled my ass as we waited in line to purchase lift tickets and arrange rental equipment for me and Helmut. Jillian's gear was in the back of the Jag.

"So how are we going to do this?" she asked. "You want to see about lessons for Helmut?" She pointed to a sign for the ski school.

I turned to her and cocked my head. "I thought I'd teach him."

"Oh," she said. "Okay."

After I'd paid for everything, we gathered Helmut from where we'd left him in his earbuds.

"You ready to snowboard?" I clapped him on the back.

He shrugged.

Jillian looked at me, adjusted her knit hat. "I'm gonna pee and then I'll meet you at the car."

"Sure," I agreed. "Let's go get our gear," I said to Helmut. He followed me to the rental check-out.

At the Jag, Jillian suited up in about four minutes, her skis over her shoulder before Helmut had gotten into the waterproof bibs I'd bought him at REI earlier in the week.

"You can go ahead," I told her. "Maybe you want to warm up. We can meet you somewhere in half an hour."

"It's okay," she said. "I'll wait for you."

Helmut squeezed sunblock onto his fingertips. "It's pretty cold," he said, rubbing the white lotion over the bridge of his nose.

"That's why I got you all that gear. You won't be cold at all once you suit up." I wrestled into my parka.

Jillian turned away from us to face the mountain, and I turned briefly to face the fine shape of things held so beautifully in her tight white ski pants.

"Dad, these don't fit." Helmut had his foot halfway into a boot.

"You've gotta loosen the laces here." I jerked the lower laces loose and his foot dropped into place. "Here, try it with that one." I handed the second boot to him.

Jillian shifted her weight, her left cheek tensing up to a perfect firmness.

"You ready?" I asked Helmut as he stood up, boot-clad and parka-wrapped, topped with a helmet and goggles.

"I guess." He fidgeted with a zipper.

I handed him his rental board.

"Let's get this road on the show." I stepped away from the SUV, clicked the lock on the key fob, and felt my left knee twinge, reminding me of days long gone on the football field.

"Jillian, how'd you learn to ski?"

Jillian gave me an odd glance, lifted an eyebrow, dropped her eyes to my crotch and grinned.

"Learned when I was a kid. My parents ski. They taught me. It's a good sport for kids." She elbowed Helmut. "You're gonna like this."

At the base of the almost-flat beginners' hill, I dropped my board and flopped into the snow.

"Let me show you how the gear works first," I said to Helmut. "So once you're off the chairlift, you'll sit down like this and strap your boots into the bindings like this." I demonstrated.

Jillian looked up the mountain, surveying the various lifts. She'd stuck her skis in the snow beside her and was adjusting her gloves without glancing down at them.

"Hey, would you mind if I took a few runs? You guys can get acclimated down here and I'll go play for a bit?"

Above me, the lifts carouseled chairs around and sent their eager occupants up the mountain. A ski-school group gathered down the slope. A thirty-something National Ski Patrol bum with a dark tan slid past. Jillian smiled and he returned the favor. She pulled a ski out of the snow and dropped it flat in front of her, then knocked snow off a boot and stuck that foot in the binding.

"Sure," I said, "go warm up. Have some fun. We'll get our legs under us here."

"I'll find you down here in an hour." She clicked the second boot into place. "I've got my phone with me." She pushed off toward a lift to my left.

Helmut watched her and sighed. "An hour?"

"It's gonna go fast."

I went over some basics with him, got him into the bindings, and tried to get him rolling onto his belly to push up to standing on the board. The hour did go by fast but included only one run. It also included two falls at the base of the chairlift as we tried to load, a fall at the top of the chairlift as we tried to disembark, and innumerable falls on the way down the imperceptibly inclined hill.

"I think I sprained my wrist." Helmut was holding his right arm out to me when Jillian skidded up. "It hurts. I fell on it."

I wasn't sure I would have called it a fall. It was perhaps more like taking a seat in the snow. I debated.

"You're okay, buddy. It'll be fine. Why don't we go get a bottle of water, take a breather, and try again? You want to get some water, Jills?"

Jillian's sunglasses reflected my question back at me, and she pursed her lips, making me think of them wrapping around my dick. And I thought about the hot tub. I felt ready for the hot tub.

"I'm okay. How about we meet up again in another hour?"

"Sure, we'll meet you down here. Maybe we can get some lunch then."

"Lunch?" She pushed off toward the lift, obviously not interested in wasting time on things like lunch when the mountain waited.

Helmut had dropped into the snow and was removing his boots from the bindings.

"I don't feel good, Dad."

"We'll get some water. You'll feel better."

I extended a hand and pulled him up. He weighed perhaps a hundred ten pounds. We lumbered toward the chalet. About halfway there, he stopped and doubled over, hands on his knees.

"I can't breathe. I think I have altitude sickness."

"You're dehydrated. We'll get you some water."

He straightened up and didn't persist with the altitude sickness and followed me through a group of grade schoolers wearing matching ski-school vests. In the chalet, I purchased water bottles, returning to the table at which I'd left him to find him on his phone, playing some sort of sniper game.

"Feeling better?" I set a bottle in front of him.

"No, I can't breathe right." He didn't move his eyes from the screen.

"You'll feel better after you rehydrate."

I dropped onto the bench opposite him, twisting the top off my own bottle.

He didn't open his water bottle. He just kept tapping the screen.

"You can go do it some more," he said after a few dozen more taps. "I can stay here and rest. Maybe I'll acclimate to the altitude."

I finished my water and crushed the bottle.

Outside, I checked a sign with a trail map and picked out a lift leading to a series of longish green-marked runs—doable runs. I schlepped toward it. On the way up, I watched people glide by beneath me, watched a guy hop off a hillock of snow into the air, touching the front edge of his snowboard with a bulky glove. At the top of the chairlift, I slid off without incident and dropped into the snow to secure my bindings. On the way down the green-rated chute, I didn't bother much with admiring the trees or anything. The snow felt icy and I had to concentrate to keep the board pointed downhill and carrying me properly. Toward the bottom, a patch of slush caught me anyway and I face-planted. The connective tissue that had held me together for fifty-one years complained loudly, creaking and popping as I struggled to my knees and got situated to flip properly onto my belly to try to rise up onto the board again to finish the run.

A woman stopped, handsome in turquoise pants and a silver helmet.

"You all right?" she asked. "I saw what happened. That ice got you bad. You need a hand up?"

"Thanks, but I've got it. I do appreciate your offer though."

She smiled and waved a ski pole and continued down the hill.

At the base of the run, I flopped into the snow to stop completely, and I unlatched my bindings and dropped my board into a rack to go find Helmut. He was sitting where I'd left him, with his phone in front of him. The only change being that he'd switched from the sniper game to surfing through Imgur memes and videos.

"You feeling better?" I dropped down across from him.

"No, my stomach hurts."

I pulled off my gloves and looked at my watch. Fifteen minutes before we could expect Jillian.

"I'm going to get some more water." I pushed myself up.

Helmut nodded, and then he laughed at a meme, and I dropped my gloves on the table in front of him and hobbled down the hallway toward a vending machine. When I got back, I held a water bottle out to Helmut.

"What do you think? Would you like to try the ski school? I saw some of the groups out there and it looks pretty cool."

Eyes on his screen, my son shook his head. "My wrist is killing me and I think I'm going to throw up."

"If you have some water and get back out into the fresh air, you'll be fine."

"No, I think I need oxygen. I heard a couple guys talking about it while you were out there. They sell bottles of oxygen in the shop. It helps with altitude sickness."

"I don't think you need oxygen."

"I texted mom. She googled it and agrees I should get some oxygen. She said for me to call her and she'd give the shop a credit-card number if you won't buy it for me."

I removed my helmet and dropped it next to my gloves, then ran a hand through my hair. I pinched the bridge of my nose. It was almost $700 for the three-day lift tickets. It was $560 for Helmut's snow gear at REI. Now I was quibbling over a twenty-dollar can of air? But it was far more than just a can of air. It was a can of quitting.

"Here." I unzipped the small chest pocket of my parka and fished out my wallet. I handed Helmut forty dollars. "Go get whatever you need. I'm going to look for Jillian. I'll meet you back here."

As I stepped out of the chalet, I saw her immediately: a white streak of graceful speed surfing down a line of moguls beneath a chairlift marked with warnings and black diamonds. Jillian. I tried to remember what it felt like to have that creature beneath me this morning, but from my vantage point in front of the chalet's deck, it was like she was soaring far above me. She skidded to a perfect stop in front of the chalet and popped out of her bindings. I walked over.

"Hey, beautiful. You looked pretty damn impressive just now."

"Oh, hey, babes. I didn't see you." She reached up and offered me a tiny peck on the lips. "How was it? How's Helmut like it?"

"It's been okay," I lied. "Little bit of a rough start. You know how it goes."

"Yeah, it's hard to get going. It takes three rough days for it to click, but he'll get it."

"You want some water or a snack?" I put my hand on her back as we walked toward the chalet's main entrance.

"I'll take some water."

As we trundled through the chalet toward Helmut's table, Jillian described the "epic beauty" of the top of the mountain: the blue sky and the "sugar-coated" trees and the fresh powder. She sounded happy, alive, self-possessed.

"Hey, what's with the oxygen, Helms?" She patted my son's back as we reached the table.

Helmut sat sucking the canister of oxygen, his phone in his free hand, a social-media app open. He removed the bottle from his mouth.

"Altitude sickness. My mom told me to buy this oxygen and use it."

Jillian caught my eye over Helmut's head.

"It's probably not altitude sickness, kiddo," she assured him. "You probably just need to drink some water and get out there and play in the air."

Helmut scowled at her and stuck the canister back in his mouth.

"Where's my change, buddy?" I teased him.

"Here." He pulled out $1.26.

"Where's the rest?" I knew the air didn't cost $38.74.

"Spent it."

I glanced at the table and saw the Sobe, Takis, Famous Amos, Mountain Dew. Jillian shook her head.

"Well, you're all fueled up and gassed up—you want to give 'er another go?" I waited for my son to look up from his phone.

"No, Dad, really, that wouldn't be smart. I'm nauseous."

"I'm gonna go get some water," Jillian said and headed down the hall.

"Here, I'll get it for you." I walked beside her toward the vending machine.

"He's not sick," Jillian whispered. "That's a classic case of big-wave sickness. Waves start pounding in and a lot of blowhard surfers get sick, you know?"

No, despite living most of my life within an hour's drive of the Gulf of Mexico, I hadn't the foggiest sense of surfing or the feigned illnesses of surfers.

"You've gotta prod him a little. Get him back out there." She patted my arm and then walked up to the vending machine. I stepped beside her and fed two dollar bills into the machine. She retrieved her water.

I sighed. "He just had a slow start. He'll get it."

"He'll get it if you push him to get it."

We walked back toward Helmut.

At the table, Jillian sat for about two minutes, polishing off her water and then putting her gloves back on.

"Well, if Helmut's out for a while, do you want to ride with me? We can do something long and gentle and scenic. It'll be nice." She gave me a look that was one part desire to ski and one part just desire, and I wanted to walk out to the Jag, throw everyone and everything in it, and get off this damned mountain and back to my private $519-a-night hot tub and room-service champagne and strawberries.

"Come on, sweetheart," she continued, "Helmut'll be fine here for a bit." She patted his arm. "Would that be cool? If your dad and I went for a bit?"

"That's fine." Helmut pulled his arm away from her.

And then I remembered the sympathy in the eyes of the woman in the turquoise pants who'd stopped to see if I was all right when I fell.

"Honey, I think I better stay with him. He almost threw up earlier, and he's eaten all this junk now. If he does have a touch of altitude sickness, I don't want him here alone. You go ski some more and maybe we can go together this afternoon."

Jillian's eyes were already back behind her goggles, and she just shrugged and turned toward the door. "Okay. I'll check in in an hour or so."

"Why'd you stay?" Helmut looked up from his phone for the first time.

"I'm worried about you," I lied—again—something in me recoiling in horror as I had to admit to myself what I was doing.

Helmut snorted and returned to the glow of the screen.

We sat together in the lodge for three and a half more hours as Jillian Grover rode her blue squares and black diamonds. At first, I tried to talk to Helmut, asked him about school and about the science fair he'd entered with a project related to refineries. I even asked him why he hadn't asked me about refining or to help him set up the project. He just grunted and shrugged. Again.

When Jillian returned from her last runs and conceded she'd sucked enough marrow from the day and felt ready to return to the resort, we piled into the Jag and headed down the switchbacks toward Santa Fe in silence.

After dinner, I finally had my crack at the hot tub, stripping naked and stepping into the hot water and letting altitude sickness and my ex-wife's credit-card number and sympathetic women in turquoise pants melt in the satisfyingly scalding pool. I shut my eyes and allowed my head to loll back and inhaled the piñon-scented air that made the eight-thousand-foot height of the place smell like a collaboration between Currier and Ives and George Catlin.

"You look content, babes." Jillian stepped onto the deck and I regretted resenting the intrusion.

"It feels great," I lied . . . yet again. The day had been flush with fibs. What I was feeling was far more complex, and satisfying, than "great."

"You want some company?"

"Absolutely." *Another* lie.

She stepped into the pool, and I noticed for the first time that she'd waxed thoroughly before the trip. Somehow, it just hadn't registered before. Noticing it now made me stir and made the sublimity of the night recede and become more bearable, easier to translate. As I hardened, the world ceased being transcendent.

Jillian floated toward me and settled next to me, taking my cock in her hand. We sat in silence for a while, the constellations settled into their places overhead for the night.

"What a great day, huh?" She ran her thumb over the tip of my dick.

"It had its ups and downs." I let myself get stupid in her hand.

"Yeah, I forgot. You had the altitude sickness to deal with." Her tone made me sit up a little, but it wasn't enough to make me pull away from her. Maybe I should have.

"He was pretty ill."

"I'm sure he was."

Now I did reach into the water and I took her hand off me.

"What?" She screwed her eyes into mine. "I'm sorry. I just think he was playing you a bit."

Neither of us said anything else. She simply ducked under the water and her tongue found me and I let her lick in long, lazy circles around me. When she came up for air, I grabbed her by the hair and pulled her head back, her spine arching, and I found my way inside her and it felt good to hear her moan. It felt very good to hear her grunt when I yanked her hair a little more, and then I had her out of the pool and on her hands and knees on the carpet of the room, just inside the patio door, and she was shuddering and constricting around me, and it felt very, very good to yank her head back and hear her whimper.

Afterward, she lay on her side against me, a nipple pushed into my armpit, and she told me how much she loved me and the night started feeling sublime again. It was lying like that, knowing how that had felt, that made dropping her at the bus station, so she could go to Taos and ski some more, all the harder three days of altitude sickness later.

Hunger

"She doesn't look well," Katy says, gesturing at my cat.

"I haven't felt well . . . been rather low," I reply.

"Depressed?" Katy's eyes hold mine. She knows my secret.

I nod.

The cat is far more affectionate when she is hungry. I find red and orange yarn bits—the colors of a missing sock—in the litterbox the next day.

Rings

Darryl watched the dark road and Mallory watched the screen of her phone, with the blue ball slipping down Maple Haven Court.

"Turn left at the next one," Mallory said. "Okay," she continued a moment later, eyes shifting from the screen to the spiral-bound book spread across her lap, shadowy in the last light of the day. "What do you think your partner's convictions about sexual intercourse are?"

"What?" Darryl turned left at the next street.

"What do you think I think about sex?"

"You fucking like it? I don't know."

"Darryl, stop it. Take this seriously. Seriously."

"How long do I stay on this one? Where do I turn?"

"Don't change the subject. Are you paying attention at all? We are supposed to have all this filled out. What do you think I think of sex?"

"Mallory, I don't know. What do you think of sex?"

"Turn here."

Darryl turned.

"Sex," Mallory insisted.

"My wife believes sex is important."

Mallory dug the pen into the upper right corner of the pre-marital-counseling worksheet.

"Turn!" She heard the edge in her voice and the volume of her command.

Darryl drove through the intersection.

"That's where you were supposed to turn," Mallory said.

"Why don't we just use the GPS?" Darryl asked.

"Why don't you take this shit seriously?"

The little gray Chevy seemed to get damp and chilly, and Darryl wished he could reach over and turn the radio on, but that wouldn't have helped anything. He made a U-turn at the next intersection. Then he turned at the corner he'd missed before.

"Okay, up here on the right," Mallory said. "Hopefully, we don't have to turn this shit in or anything."

"It's fine, Mallory. What are they going to do? Tell us we can't get married? Mallory, we've been married for three months. I don't even know why we're doing this."

"We're doing this because it's important. I don't get why you can't see how much this means. I don't get why you don't get that."

"I don't get it because we're married, Mallory. We're married and you don't go to church, so I don't understand why you give a fuck about any of this."

"Why I give a fuck? Darryl, you just don't get it."

"No, I don't get it."

"Here. Park. It's number fourteen fifty-two." Mallory gestured out the window at the white rectangles painted on the curb, boxing in square, stenciled, black numerals.

"It looks like your mom's house," Darryl said.

"Okay, here's your book." Mallory twisted in her seat and grabbed another spiral-bound book off the back seat. "Here." She dropped it into Darryl's lap as he lifted the parking brake.

He removed the key from the ignition. The Chevy Spark had cost the couple nine grand two years ago and still used a real key in a real ignition switch, and a manual transmission that Mallory, even after two years, struggled to drive.

"Take your ring off," Mallory said to Darryl, slipping her own wedding band off and dropping it in the plastic, molded cup holder in front of the stick shift.

"Are you serious?"

"Yes, I'm serious, Darryl. Take your fucking ring off. Don't you get it? We're not married, Darryl. These people don't know we're married. To them, we're not married. Until we get married in the Church, you can't talk about us being married."

Darryl slipped off his ring and put it in a hip pocket.

"What are these people's names again?" he asked his wife as she stuffed her workbook into an Old Navy tote.

"James and Mary Breem."

"James and Mary. James and Mary. Okay, James and Mary."

Mallory flipped the visor down and applied lipstick, focusing on the mirror.

Darryl waited.

His wife dug in her purse for a comb.

Darryl bent back the upper corner of his *For Better and For Ever: A Resource for Couples Preparing for Christian Marriage* workbook. He creased it and dug his thumbnail down over the crease. Mallory flipped the mirror's plastic cover down and flipped the passenger-side visor up.

"Ready?" Darryl looked at her.

She opened her door and the heels of her Massimo Matteos sank into the grass and dirt as she struggled out of the car.

"James and Mary," Darryl repeated as he walked around the rear of the Spark and proffered a hand to Mallory.

On the brick ranch's stoop, Mallory pointed to the doorbell. "Ring it."

Darryl pressed the just-barely-lit-up, sort-of-orange button, and the couple listened to the chimes on the other side of the door.

"Welcome," Mary Breem said a few beats later, holding her arms out and offering Mallory a hug. "And congratulations! This is such an exciting and happy time, isn't it? Come in. Come in. Here, we'll go right into the living room. Make yourselves comfortable. Jim, the kids from St. Monica's are here. Jim, honey, where'd you go?"

A man who looked about old enough to be Darryl's or Mallory's father, and who likely hadn't been to the gym since Darryl and Mallory truly were kids, walked into the living room from an overstuffed, worn-out, champagne-hued dining room. He wore a gray sweater, with a contrasting placket and snaps, and argyle socks with gold thread across the toes. The two couples took seats around a living room of 1990s décor and tired tochieres, Jesus, with His Sacred Heart, and His Immaculate Mother looking on.

"Well, thank you so much for volunteering to do our marriage prep with us," Mallory said, focusing mostly on Mrs. Breem.

"We're glad to," Mrs. Breem responded, a hand patting her husband's knee. "Would you like anything? A beer, cheese, crackers? We just opened an Alamos Red Blend if you'd like some wine."

"I've got a bunch of Shiners in the fridge," James Breem offered.

Mallory looked at Darryl on the couch beside her. She matched Mary Breem's placement of a hand on her husband's knee.

"Um," Mallory started, "the wine sounds nice. I'll take a glass of wine. Beer, baby?"

"A Shiner would be great," Darryl said. He had a hand on the arm of the brick-colored couch, his fingers kind of digging into the brocade upholstery.

The Breems rose and turned a corner toward the kitchen. Darryl and Mallory didn't speak. Mallory's feet rocked on the Massimo

Matteos' heels, which had again sunk, this time into the almost-shag pile of the chai-colored carpet. Darryl studied the ceiling plaster, the fingers of the hand not on the couch arm playing with the pages of his marriage-prep workbook.

Mary Breem returned with two glasses of the cheap red blend, and James handed an already sweaty bottle of Shiner Bock to Darryl.

"So how long have you been members at St. Monica's?" Mary asked.

Mallory pulled in her feet, gathered them at right angles under her knees. "We're, um, not members of the parish yet. But we've been going for a while now. What, baby, like a year, year and a half? We just haven't signed up or anything yet. But we love it there."

"Oh, that's fine," Mary Breem replied. "Stephanie in the office can get you the paperwork, so you can sign up and get your envelopes and get on the mailing lists. We've got so many wonderful ministries. We'd love to get you more involved. I lead a prison ministry and you might love the hand-chime ministry. James is in that. He says it's a lot of fun. Great group of people. Right, James? And maybe Darryl would like to become a Knight. We have a thriving Knights of Columbus council. James can help with exploring that as well."

"I'd love to get more involved," Mallory said. "I do the Zumba classes on Thursdays. But I'd love to get more involved with other things."

Darryl rested his head on the hand attached to the arm he'd set on the couch's armrest.

"My sister does the Zumba classes. She loves Grace's dance routines. Loves the classes," Mary Breem said. "She's into all the Latin music. She listens to a lot of Ricky Martin."

Mallory nodded and rubbed Darryl's knee. Darryl held the Shiner bottle to his lips for several swallows of beer. A clock in the hallway between the living room and kitchen clicked.

"Well, let's start with a prayer," Mrs. Breem said. "In the name of the Father, and the Son, and the Holy Spirit."

She crossed herself and looked at the open book in her lap, reading a prayer from it while her husband followed with the book he held, and Mallory and Darryl stared at their respective knees.

"Amen." Mary Breem looked up. "So, when's the wedding date?" she asked.

"Oh, we haven't set one yet," Mallory answered. "We don't want to rush. We've met with Deacon Frank a couple times, and we went through the pre-marriage questionnaire. We figured we'd get these sessions going with you and get our paperwork together—we still haven't gotten our baptismal certificates and stuff—and then we'd figure out a date. Darryl's dad lives in Akron, so he'll have to travel. My dad's in Sacramento, but he probably won't come. But we need to see what dates could be good for them. Just in case. That kind of stuff."

"Do you know where you want to have the reception?" Mrs. Breem seemed like a cheerful person.

"We're still debating," Mallory answered. "There's the University Club and Corinthian Yacht Club and the art museum. My mom and I are taking a tour of venues on the sixteenth."

"So your mother is local?" Mary Breem asked.

"Yes, she's just over in East."

"That's nice," Mrs. Breem responded. "So your parents are divorced?"

"Yes," Mallory answered, her eyes darting to her left to look at Darryl for an instant. "Both our parents are divorced." She looked back at Mary Breem. "I mean, we both have divorced parents."

"Well, that might be a good place to start." Mary Breem patted the open workbook in her lap. "Did you look at Chapter Two? Have you talked together about your parents' divorces and how they may have affected your perceptions of marriage?"

Mallory turned to her husband, who had the Shiner to his lips at that moment.

"We did," Mallory said, brushing her hand over her workbook. Still looking at Darryl, she continued, "We talked about where we grew up and our families and our parents' habits."

"Great," Mary Breem said. "Now, we're not going to ask you to read your answers to the questions at the end of the chapter or anything—those are for the two of you to discuss—but did anything come up as you worked through them that you want to discuss?"

"Not really," Mallory said. "I think it all made sense, you know."

"What about you, Darryl?" Mrs. Breem leaned forward on her couch and gave Darryl a smile, like she wanted to smile him away from the Shiner Bock and out of the corner of his and Mallory's couch, where he seemed to have sunk. Like his wife's high heels in the carpet.

Darryl swiveled his head toward Mallory and then glanced at James and then Mary Breem.

"Um, yeah, we went through everything. And it made sense. Um, we talked about how my dad and I don't have the best relationship. Like we aren't too close. Mallory's a lot closer to her parents than I am.

Than like I'm close to my parents. Like her dad gave us money for the house. I mean—"

Mallory leaned into her husband and pushed her elbow into his upper arm, swinging her hair and grinning toward the Breems.

"Yeah, I'm really lucky," she said. "My dad gave us a big check to put into savings, so we'd have money to buy a house once we get married. We want to buy something around Pinebrooke."

"Oh, that's nice over there." Mary Breem took a sip of wine. It looked like she tried to catch James's eye over the rim of the wineglass as she drank.

James stopped picking at the label of his beer bottle. "So where are you each living now?" he asked.

Mallory offered her mother's neighborhood immediately, naming her mother's street. She buried a hand between her leg and Darryl's leg and tried to poke him without getting noticed.

"And what about you, Darryl? Close by? And let me know when you need another one." James used his bottle to point at Darryl's beer.

"Oh, I'm good right now. Thanks. I'm over off Orchard View. I, uh, share a house over there with a buddy."

"Orchard View? That's close to church. And that's close to Pinebrooke—so you want to stay in that neighborhood after the wedding?" Mary Breem ran her hand over the arm of her couch.

"Yeah," Mallory answered, "Darryl likes it over there. We don't want to move far. It's a nice area. I'm looking forward to living over there. And the schools are good. The kids will be able to walk to Brookfield Elementary."

"Oh, that reminds me." Mary Breem patted the book in her lap. "Has anyone talked to you about NFP classes? Helped you find one that works for your schedules? There are a few to choose from."

"Not yet," Mallory replied. "We, um, we hadn't looked yet."

"Well," Mary Breem pushed herself off the couch, "let me go get Sunday's bulletin. I'm pretty sure there was one listed in there. One minute."

Mallory and Darryl watched Mary Breem rise from the couch. They watched James watch his wife turn the corner and disappear in the direction of the kitchen. Darryl took a sip of beer just as James raised his bottle to his lips. Mallory swished the wine in her glass.

"It's really cozy in here," she said. "You have a nice house. Or living room, at least." She pulled a laugh up from somewhere.

"Mary keeps us real comfortable," James said. "I'm a lucky man. You both raised Catholic?"

"No," Mallory said. "Darryl's parents are Methodist. I converted in college. My parents are kinda hippies. I grew up pretty New Age-y, but I got involved with a Catholic group on campus when I was a freshman and ended up converting."

"I was right." Mrs. Breem's voice preceded her around the corner. "There's an ad in here. There're a couple programs coming up. I'll give this to you to take in case you don't have yours from Sunday. It's a start at least."

She returned to the living room and walked over to Mallory and Darryl's couch and held the bulletin out. Mallory's smile looked a little crooked to Darryl, who watched his wife take the thin newsletter.

"Now, where were we, honey? I'm sorry. But I wanted to remember to ask about the NFP thing before we got too far. Are either of you familiar with the science behind natural family planning? Have either of you—"

"Honey," James interrupted his wife, "they'll get all that when they take the family-planning class. I don't think we need to worry about it now."

"You're right," Mary Breem agreed. "I'm getting off track. We've got two chapters to cover."

She reinstalled the workbook on her lap after returning to the couch.

"Now, should we just go ahead and look at Chapter One?" Mary Breem glanced at Darryl and Mallory and then at her husband. Darryl watched her eyes instead of taking a drink—because he didn't want his beer to go away too quickly.

"Sure," Mallory answered. "We went through that at home."

Darryl lifted the Shiner bottle to his lips—took a small sip—as he pushed his thumb into his wife's thigh. *At home.* At *their* home.

Mallory swiveled her head toward him. She wondered if he was grinning around the mouth of the bottle. She cocked her head and then continued.

"We went over all that. We talked about our wedding plans. We've got the list of documents we need to get for Deacon Frank. I was baptized in college, so I can just call that parish and get all my records. Darryl still needs to talk to his mom about getting his baptismal certificate or whatever the Methodist Church has. It's not a big deal, though. We'll get all that together."

"Okay, great." Mary Breem turned a page in her workbook.

Mallory took another sip of wine. The clock in the hall made another sound.

"Chapter Two, like we said, goes into your families," Mary Breem said. "Your parents and siblings. Anything stand out? Any big family concerns? You've been the quiet one, Darryl. Where'd you grow up?"

Mallory turned to Darryl and watched him as he sat up a little and as he placed the beer bottle on the end table beside the couch.

"I was born in Cleveland. But my folks got divorced when I was six. My mom grew up down here, so after the divorce, she moved me and my older sister to Beaumont to be close to my grandparents. I grew up over there."

"And you said you're not close to your dad?" Mary Breem looked motherly when she asked.

"Uh uh. But my mom and I are tight and I'm still pretty close to my sister. She's two years older. She's in San Antonio now. But we still see each other pretty regularly."

"Lisa—that's Darryl's sister's name—she and her boyfriend met us in San Marcos last summer to float the river," Mallory said. "We had a great time. We spent the weekend together. Lisa's very cool. She's going to be one of my bridesmaids."

"That's great," Mary Breem said. "It's always so positive when the bride and groom get along with one another's families.

"Yeah, and Lisa and I are pretty close," Mallory added.

Mallory and Mary Breem worked through Chapter Two of the book. James got fresh beers for himself and Darryl and even refilled the women's wineglasses with the bottle of Alamos. Mallory read from the lists she had made in the workbook on the drive over, and Darryl chipped in when he had to. When the couples came to a mutual, unuttered understanding that they had spent enough time on the workbook and lists, James shifted in his chair. He lowered the ankle that had rested on the knee of its opposite.

"You done there, sweetheart?" he asked Mary Breem.

She nodded and handed her empty wineglass to her husband.

"Mallory? Darryl?" James rose and stepped to the couch, stood over Mallory and Darryl.

Mallory nodded as Mary Breem had and handed the older man her glass. Then she reached out and over her surreptitious husband and took Darryl's bottles off the end table and handed them up.

James disappeared to the kitchen with the collection of glasses and bottles, and Mary Breem asked whether Mallory or Darryl had any questions. She asked when they would be free for another session.

"How about two weeks from Wednesday?" Mallory responded. "That would work, right, honey?" She put a hand on Darryl's arm, then dropped it to his knee.

"Sure," Darryl replied. "Works for me." He rubbed the tops of this thighs, his right hand bumping Mallory's hand now resting on his knee.

When James returned from the kitchen, Mary Breem asked Mallory and Darryl if they would like to close the session with prayer. She held up the workbook from her lap.

"We've got this little closing prayer here for the engaged couple to recite." She twisted the workbook for Mallory and Darryl to see the page.

"Oh, perfect," Mallory said, first squinting at Mary Breem's book and then opening her own to the page with the prayers.

"In the name of the Father, and of the Son, and of the Holy Spirit." Mallory crossed herself and began reciting the brief prayer.

"Amen," Mallory and the Breems said when she'd reached the end of the prayer.

Mallory squeezed Darryl's knee. Then patted it again. She slipped her workbook into her tote and everyone rose. Mallory hugged the Breems. Darryl shook hands. Mary Breem opened the front door and told the younger couple to be careful driving. She waved as Darryl and Mallory walked to their car parked at the curb, plastic solar lights dug into the grass along the concrete path lighting the way. Darryl unlocked the Chevy and opened Mallory's door for her, waiting for her to tuck the Massimo Matteos into the footwell before closing her in. He walked around the front of the Spark and let himself in his door, buckling his seatbelt across his lap after he'd settled in. And then he reached into his pocket, swiveling in his seat a little to get his hand into the fabric.

"Huh," he said.

"What's that?" Mallory didn't turn to her husband. She was digging in her purse.

"Nothing," Darryl said. He put the car in gear and edged it away from the curb, beginning a U-turn in the street.

At the intersection, he turned right, retracing the steps he and Mallory had argued over on the way to the Breems' home. Mallory checked her phone and returned a text from her sister. Then she began the process of checking her social-media feeds.

"Sweetheart, Gwen and Steve are having a barbeque on Saturday. She says we don't have to bring anything, unless there's something special we want to drink. Josie and Paul have already confirmed they're going."

"Okay," Darryl said.

"You don't want to go?"

"No, that's fine. Sounds good. I'll take some of that new Southern Star IPA." Darryl stopped at the red light at the mouth of the subdivision.

"You don't sound excited."

"No, I am. I get along with Steve and Paul fine."

Mallory returned to her phone. After checking her physical-activity record for the day and her work email, she darkened the screen.

"Well," she shifted in her seat, adjusting her seatbelt and twisting her hips to face her husband, "what did you think?"

"Of the prep thing? It was fine." Darryl watched the street lights slide past.

Mallory fingered the hem of her blouse. "Do you want to discuss anything? Did any of the points that came up spark anything for you?" She wrapped a strand of hair around an index finger.

"Um, not really."

"Really? Nothing?"

"Nothing jumps to mind."

"Do you think your sister would be a bridesmaid when we get married in the Church?"

"Lisa?" Darryl glanced at his wife. "I don't know. Probably."

"Do you think she'd think it's weird?"

Darryl tapped the steering wheel with his fingers. "Mallory, *I* think it's weird. Lisa probably will too."

"Why do you think it's weird?" Mallory didn't speak loudly, and she straightened herself out in her seat and rubbed the fabric over her thighs as she asked.

"Mallory, I've already said it. A couple times. This isn't us. This just doesn't feel like us. At all."

"I was Catholic when you met me."

"You'd joined some Catholic club at school. Okay, you were Catholic. But it's not like you went to church."

"I go now."

"You go to Zumba once a week. Mallory, we've never been to Mass."

"I went at Christmas. And I went last summer."

"Okay, you went to Mass at Christmas. And like twice in June."

Mallory inhaled and then fidgeted with the phone-charging cord. "This means a lot to me."

"I know. That's why I'm doing it."

Mallory wound the cord around her finger and then unwound it and then wound it again.

In the couple's driveway, Darryl set the parking brake and killed the engine, opened his door. He stepped out and then turned and bent over the driver's seat and then the floor mat.

Mallory grabbed her purse and the Old Navy bag with her workbook in it and slipped out of the vehicle. "What's wrong, honey? What're you looking for?"

"Oh, I'm fine." Darryl lifted the floor mat and ran a hand under it. He looked up at his wife after setting the mat back in place. "Don't worry about it. I'll be right in."

Mallory shrugged and walked toward the front door.

"Find what you were looking for?" she asked from the couch several minutes later when Darryl came into the house.

"Uh uh," he said, taking off his jacket and shaking out the pockets.

"Well, what did you lose?"

Darryl hesitated. "I can't find my ring."

"What?" Mallory muted the TV.

"I put my wedding ring in my pocket when we went into the Breems' place. I didn't feel it when we got into the car and now I can't find it."

"Darryl!" Mallory didn't say anything else for a breath. Then she pushed the fleece blanket off her lap. "I need to get mine."

"Yours is right here." Darryl held out the gold ring. "I found it in the console when I was looking for mine."

Mallory jumped off the couch. "Here." She took the ring from her husband and settled it on her finger against her engagement ring.

"I can't believe you lost yours."

"I'm sorry." Darryl walked past his wife and toward the kitchen and a beer. "I'm sure I'll find it in the car in the morning. When I can see in there. It's just too damn dark now."

"You aren't going to find it. It's probably in the Breems' couch cushions or something. Great, now I'm going to have to ask them if I can ransack their couch for the wedding ring you've been carrying in anticipation of the wedding."

From the kitchen, where he stood in front of the open fridge, Darryl didn't respond. Mallory dropped back on the couch and wrapped the blanket around herself.

"I can ask to check their couch next time we're there," Darryl said when he walked out of the kitchen with a bottle of IPA a few beats later. "Or I can email them tomorrow. It'll turn up."

"No, don't email them. I'll call them. I'll figure out something to say."

"There's nothing to figure out, Mallory. Just tell them your husband lost his wedding ring."

"We're not married, Darryl. We're not fucking married."

"We're married, Mallory. That's why I have a wedding ring. If you don't think we're married, why'd we even get married?"

"I don't know." Mallory twisted the blanket over her forearms. "I wanted to go to Cozumel with you? I wanted to buy the house with you? I don't know." She stared at the beige fleece.

"You know, the priest is gonna know we're married when you can't come up with a marriage license. The state's not gonna issue you a license to marry your current husband."

Mallory got off the couch and walked toward the stairs. Darryl unmuted the television, changed the channel. He took a sip of beer.

Mallory was in bed in the dark when he went upstairs an hour later. She listened to the sounds from the bathroom: the Waterpik and then Darryl's Sonicare.

"You okay?" Darryl slipped into bed and wrapped himself against his wife's back.

Mallory shut her eyes.

"We'll find the ring," Darryl said. "I'm not worried."

"You don't care."

"I do care. I care a lot."

"No, you don't care about the Church and getting married in the Church and doing things right. You don't take anything seriously."

"Mallory, I do care, but this isn't us. This isn't you."

"Darryl, it is me. It's totally me. It's what I want. So badly."

"What do you want?"

"To really be married. And we aren't."

"I think we're married."

"I don't."

"Why not?"

Beneath the blanket and comforter, Mallory scooched away from her husband. She waited to feel sleepy, waited to feel safe or happy or content or peaceful, waited for something. She waited for *it* to feel the way it was *supposed* to feel, waited to feel like *she* was *supposed* to feel. She'd been waiting a while now, months now, years now. And she still didn't feel it. She didn't feel it that night, like she hadn't felt it the night before, or the night they got married, or on their honeymoon in Cozumel, or the night Darryl proposed.

She waited under the covers, but nothing changed and the room just stayed dark, with slits of lighter darkness rimming each slat of the blinds of the big window facing the foot of the bed.

*

Maybe it was the dog in her lap. Or something in her eyes. Regardless, I stopped, fumbled for my wallet in my back pocket. Inside sat a lonely five.

"It's all I've got," I mumbled as I dropped the crumpled bill in the shoebox balanced on her knees beside the little dog. "God bless."

"I take credit cards," she replied before I could step away. She shoved a square device into the phone that had materialized next to the shoebox and dog.

The jury had been good to me, to my client, this afternoon, so I pulled out a Visa.

"All right," I said to this businesswoman. "Put $20 on here." I handed her the card.

The wheelchair burped a couple times and whirred loudly before it started up and rolled her away from me after she returned my card. I didn't look over my shoulder to see whether she turned into the McDonald's or the liquor store.

Especially Marty Robbins

C lassic country, the young doctor had said. He'd told Gwen to dig up a stereo and put it in the old man's room and put on music . . . classic country. The doctor had named artists, but the only one Gwen could remember was someone called Marty Robbins—because her uncle's name was Marty and her cousin (from a different uncle) was named Robin. Riding the elevator back up from the breakroom, stereo in her arms, Gwen couldn't imagine what would make someone dump an old man wearing four hundred dollars' worth of Lucchese boots on a curb in front of a hospital.

"Mr. Whittier," she called, her voice low but not a whisper, knocking on the door to the poor guy's room with a corner of the stereo after the short walk down the hall. "Mr. Whittier, it's your charge nurse. My name's Gwen. I've got some music for you."

She pushed the door open and stepped into the dark room, shivered. She'd get another blanket for the old guy next. In the bed, the hillock beneath the covers didn't move, didn't say anything, didn't let on it was still alive. On the counter behind the bed sat a cheap plastic Tupperware-knock-off box, issued by the hospital to hold patient personal effects. While the Social Security card reading "Carter Harold Whittier" that had been in the man's pocket now sat somewhere with security, the plastic box on the counter contained a safety pin and the piece of notebook paper the pin had held clipped to the man's shirt . . . with the paper's two lines of blue-ink handwriting:

My name is Carter. I'm not right.

Maybe you can help me. Thank you.

Gwen shivered again, set the stereo on the wood-veneer table on the far side of the room, groped beneath the table to plug the thing in.

"There we go," she murmured, pressing the power button and getting a red light indicating life. "Now . . . Marty Robbins."

She pulled her phone from the pocket of her scrubs and tapped and scrolled until an image of a red record-album cover with a black-clad cowboy on it appeared.

"Hmm." She sniffed, tapped a song named "The Cowboy in the Continental Suit," set the phone in the stereo's dock.

"Well, he walks out in the arena, all dressed up to the brim," sang a throaty male voice through the speakers. "Said he just came down from a place called Highland Rim."

Gwen shrugged, turned to the door to go in search of another blanket for the old fellow in the bed.

"Said he came to ride the horse, the one they call the Brute." The man in the bed sat up, pushed a cracking, liver-spotted, threadbare voice into the darkness. "But he didn't look like a cowboy in that continental suit," he sang over the stereo, over the guitar melody.

"Mr. Whittier?" Gwen walked to the railing that ran around the bed, glanced at the screens of vital signs and indicators of mortality. "How are you doing, Mr. Whittier?" She stepped to a cart bearing a laptop, opened the computer, and typed in a note to go with the others, to go with the story of an old man stumbling into the emergency room in expensive clothes and falling, bleeding from his nose, whimpering while the nurse from triage called for assistance. Never saying anything. Never showing signs of visual acuity.

"Well, we snickered at the way he dressed, but he never said a word." The old voice soared upward with that of Mr. Marty Robbins.

"Mr. Whittier, I'm your charge nurse Gwen." She patted his arm. "How are you doing?"

"He walked on by the rest of us as if he hadn't heard," Mr. Whittier sang on.

Gwen turned back to the computer, clicking in a message to the dark-eyed, dark-complected young doctor. She traveled for her assignments, hadn't been at this hospital long enough to know anyone. Dr. Malone it was, wasn't it? Looked to be about Gwen's son's age. But that couldn't be possible, could it? You couldn't get through medical school and a residency that fast, could you? No, he was just baby-faced—must just be baby-faced.

"A thousand bucks went to the man who could ride this wild cayuse." The singing continued behind Gwen. "A meaner horse was never born than the one they called the Brute." The voice broke, coughed.

Gwen stepped to the counter behind the bed. In a cupboard, she found a stack of clear plastic cups, filled one at the sink.

"Mr. Whittier, would you like some water?" She held out the cup.

"The horse that he was looking for was in chute number eight. He walked up very slowly, put his hand upon the gate." The man's eyes didn't flicker. No blink, no turn of the head.

The music continued and the old voice continued.

And the darkness around Gwen continued: continued being dark, continued being just cool enough to make her shiver yet again. Continued being the color of sadness and smelling of unloved, abandoned things.

Gwen waited, couldn't leave the old guy.

The doctor returned. Yes, she'd been right: Dr. Malone.

"Mr. Whittier." The doctor had a voice young like his face. "How are we doing, sir?"

The old man simply sang on. Stared through Dr. Malone and sang. "Underneath some ragged clothes could be a millionaire."

Dr. Malone raised a dark eyebrow at Gwen. She shrugged. "I put on the music and he just sat up and started singing."

The doctor shook his close-cropped head, pushed glasses up his too-young nose. "The boots," he said into the laptop as he entered notes, "the boots and the belt and his age. A guy that old, dressed like that—he grew up on this music. I wondered if it would be a memory."

The song ended.

"Out in the West Texas town of El Paso." Mr. Robbins began his next performance.

And Mr. Whittier wasn't a syllable behind him. "I fell in love with a Mexican girl."

Gwen shook her head. "It's a bit chilly in here, Dr. Malone. I'll get some extra blankets."

The doctor didn't say anything, just smiled, nodded.

At the nurses' station in the hall, Gwen stopped to inquire about the status of the social worker they'd requested. He was on his way, would be there within the hour. Oh, and security had checked the video footage of the area around the entry porte-cochère. Would Gwen like to see it?

The grainy (how could it be grainy in this age of television-quality video on phones?) footage showed a silver sedan pull up in front of the emergency room's automatic doors, a car non-descript in everything save a lack of license plates. A woman in high heels sliding out of the driver's seat, walking around to open the passenger door.

The old man who enjoyed outdated country music—Mr. Whittier—swaying, stumbling a bit as he struggled out of the car. The woman (so hard to make out a face, a look—maybe thirty years old, but that was based more on the long legs and short skirt that couldn't be worn much past thirty) hugging the man, reaching up and smoothing thin hair clinging to a seventy-something-year-old skull. Pinning a torn piece of notebook paper to the man's shirt. Another hug, long, the old man reaching out, tugging the woman back as she released him. The woman pushing the man toward the glass doors, gesturing, pushing again. Emphatic. Again. Hurrying back around the car, into the driver's seat. The car pulling away as the man turned right and left and then stumbled through the doors, hit the terrazzo floor . . . off camera.

Gwen shook her head.

The other nurse clicked out of the video interface, shrugged. Sad. Weird. Who would . . . ?

Back in the dark room, Marty Robbins was still singing. Mr. Whittier was still singing. Apparently, five brothers had left Arkansas in search of the man who'd murdered their pa. Oh, not just a man, Gwen learned, a gambler. She unfolded the blanket and wrapped it around bony shoulders, around a hint of kyphosis and the smell of things lost very long ago.

He smelled the way Gwen's dad had smelled at the end. Had it been twelve years? A dozen years since that sweet old cuss went to Jesus? Gwen didn't mean to presume, but she could just see her old man up there with the Good Lord, asking St. Peter if he had a truck that needed fixin' or some guns that needed cleanin' or—

The song changed and Mr. Whittier told Gwen to "come sit by my side if you love me." And then he smiled. He turned to her and smiled, wide with neat, straight teeth and a hole beneath his left eye where Gwen guessed someone had nuked off some basal cells.

"Do not hasten to bid me adieu." The old man kept grinning . . . in tune. And then he winked.

Gwen cocked her head.

"Just remember the Red River Valley," he sang. "And the cowboy that's loved you so true."

"You're sweet, old man," Gwen whispered. She'd sat beside her dad at the end, at the last, in a hospital room like this one. Reverend LeConte there with the Good Book. And Momma. Poor Momma. She hadn't lasted but ten days after that.

And then the old man reached out and took Gwen's hand. Kept singing, back to staring straight ahead into the wall across from the foot of the bed. Singing and swaying a little with the blanket around his shoulders and a soft grin.

He held her hand and asked her again to sit beside him and think of that old Red River Valley.

"Hello? Mr. Whittier?" A rap on the door jamb.

"Come in!" Gwen snuck her hand free and gave the old back a rub on the shoulder blade as she stepped away toward the door.

"I'm Hector Saenz." Another impossibly young man. This one with thick black hair and a pink tie with no sport coat. A thin, brick-colored accordion file under his arm.

He offered his hand.

Gwen took it. "I'm Gwen Abernathy. I'm the charge nurse for this floor. You're from the Aging and Disability Department?" She pointed at the file.

"Guessed right." The young man looked like he should have been in one of those music videos that plays in ads on the internet . . . with boats in the background. "So how's Mr. Whittier?"

Gwen followed the almost-boy's eyes to the old man, who hadn't stopped singing. He was on to trying to ride a wild strawberry roan, "a sun fishin' son of a gun."

"You like old country ballads, Mr. Whittier?" Hector Saenz asked the again-unseeing eyes.

"He's about the worst bucker I've seen on the range," Mr. Whittier crooned. "He'll turn on a nickel and give you some change."

Gwen gave a half smile. "He likes singing."

"Whatever makes him happy, right? May I?" Hector gestured with the file at a seat away from the stereo.

"Make yourself comfortable." Gwen crossed to the laptop. "I'll just make a few notes. And I'll message for Dr. Malone to join us."

"Of course."

When Dr. Malone stepped into the sound of a romanticized open range a few minutes later, Hector was explaining to Gwen that a Colleen Whittier had opened six cases with the county Aging and Disability Resource Center over the last eighteen months. Ostensibly the daughter. Supposedly because of the unmanageable cognitive decline of a Mr. Carter Whittier.

This Colleen had given the address of a one-bedroom rental near the mall on the west side of town as the old man's address. Hector would, in the morning, file the papers to get a court-appointed guardian. It seemed the old guy had a pension and decent Social Security income. And an annuity. Some savings in an account at Chase Bank. The title to a house on the river had passed to this Ms. Colleen Whittier two years ago. She'd sold the place three months ago. Four bedrooms, fifty-two-hundred square feet, a million and change. Not clear what had happened to the money. A trust account the guardian would have to investigate.

Hector paused. Pulled out another sheet of paper.

No driver's license, one credit card shared with Colleen, a debit card for the Chase Account (Colleen was on that account, too), a loyalty card at the Albertsons, a library card.

"Have we tried contacting Colleen?" Dr. Malone asked, wiping his glasses with the hem of his scrubs.

"I called the number from the Resource Center applications. Out of service." Hector Saenz smoothed a hand over the incongruous tie.

"The stranger there among them had a big iron on his hip," Mr. Whittier responded from the bed.

Hector turned to him. "We'll take care of you, Mr. Whittier. I'll get with the court tomorrow. We'll get you a guardian. Get access to your finances and get you placed somewhere comfortable. You'll be in good hands." He pushed himself up. "It's going to be okay." Walked to the side of the bed, put his hand on one of those blanketed, stooping shoulders. "I'll make sure we get you a good stereo, too. Lots of country. You ever hear Tom Russell? You'd like him, buddy."

Dr. Malone followed Hector Saenz out of the room, left Gwen alone with Mr. Whittier and Marty Robbins and the thought of her dad squeezing her hand at the very end, whispering "love . . . so proud . . . blessed life."

Gwen made a few last notes, turned to leave, to make her rounds of the floor.

"You're very kind, Miss Gwen," Carter Whittier whispered.

***

The sandwich place by the hospital tended to have long lines from noon onward. Till about one-thirty or so. So Dr. Malone had suggested sneaking out early, had told Gwen she had to let him take her and her colleagues Deborah and Seth out to lunch for a farewell-Gwen break. She'd be *home* tomorrow afternoon, back to her condo, to too much privacy, too much me-time. She'd be off to another assignment fast. It was better that way.

Deborah led the group to a booth by a window. Gwen slid in after her. Deborah dropped an arm around Gwen's shoulders. "We'll miss you, Gwen. You really fit in. It'll be hard to find another you."

Seth and the doctor agreed, offered the quips of people who didn't know someone so very well but would sincerely miss them. They asked about her plans, next assignment. Ran down that other hospital—the one she'd be going to. Sang the praises of going home, hoped her family would be happy to see her.

"My son moved to San Antonio two years ago. He and his fiancée will come over for Thanksgiving," Gwen offered.

Outside the window, people passed on the flagstone pathways, or sat at umbrella-shaded tables, with plastic flatware and cups, and stacks of rough brown napkins trying to escape in swirls of sun-tinged breeze. People in scrubs. Or with backpacks or briefcases.

The black plastic square Dr. Malone had carried to the table vibrated and lit up with a circle of red lights, alerted the doctor and nurses that their orders were ready at the counter on the other side of the restaurant.

"Seth and I will get everything." Dr. Malone pushed his glasses up his nose, slid out of the booth.

"So do we know what happened to that poor old fellow who got dumped in the ER in August?" Gwen asked several minutes later after working into her soup. "His name was Mr. Whittier." And she didn't know why but she suddenly remembered a night years ago when she'd seen a car ahead of hers hit a buck. The animal had leapt out of the trees beside the road and the other car hadn't had any time at all to do anything but plow into the creature. The deer had gone down on its knees and lain in the dark road, and Gwen had slowed, and then the great antlered old man had stumbled and struggled up, foreleg shattered, blood dripping, and Gwen had started crying and had felt ashamed because she couldn't stop—couldn't stop to help the other driver, who'd pulled over, couldn't stop to help the deer (if that were even possible), couldn't stop crying.

She set her spoon aside.

Dr. Malone put his turkey sandwich down, wiped his lips. "Oh, I remember him. Carter Harold Whittier." He ripped open his bag of potato chips. "That poor bloke."

"Did you hear what happened to him?" Gwen waited.

"He got a court-appointed guardian. Had quite a bit of money, I guess. Got settled in a good home." The doctor pulled out a curled yellow chip. It crunched as he bit down on it. "But I couldn't help it," he said after a moment. "A case like that just makes you think. Who would just dump an old guy like that? Especially one with money and resources? How could you just dump your dad on the curb like that? Disappear. . . . So I poked around online a little." Another chip.

He still looked so young to Gwen. His mother must have been very proud.

"Did you find anything?" Deborah asked. She could have been Gwen's daughter in build and features. "I mean, really. Who *would* dump a poor old guy like that? At least just get him a Medicaid bed or something. I can't *imagine*."

"I don't know." Seth shifted, stabbed into a plate of macaroni and cheese. "I don't think you can always tell. It's hard to judge. Maybe he abused her—like the daughter, if that is who dropped him—as a kid or something. Maybe just getting him to the hospital was a heroic effort for the chick. It's just so hard to know. I went to school with a girl whose dad abused her for years. It was weird. She couldn't walk away from him for good. He had some sort of family pull over her, but she couldn't be around him." Another bite of macaroni. "You just never know."

Dr. Malone took a sip of water. "I guess you don't." He set the cup down, spun it in his hands. "I went on Facebook and found a Colleen Whittier Horsch. Living in Cancun and selling Pampered Chef."

Deborah sniffed. "Cancun? Yeah, well, I'm guessing we know then. She took a bunch of the old man's money, so she could go live on a beach in Mexico. Poor old guy."

In Dr. Malone's hands, the plastic cup rotated 'round and 'round. "Her pictures looked something like the footage from the security camera. So I messaged her. Just asked if she had a father named Carter. I told her who I was and that I knew where her dad had ended up and that if she wanted to get in touch with him I could give her the details."

"And what did she say?" Gwen leaned slightly forward over her soup bowl. "Did she reply?"

The doctor pulled his phone out of a pocket. Tapped.

"This is all I got back." He passed the phone across the table.

Carter likes old country music. Especially Marty Robbins.

All That for Nuthin'

"It's like you don't wanna learn, Bobby." BethAnn twisted her hands in the folds of her skirt, heard the click of the handcuffs sealing around her son's wrists, watched the officers range through her home looking for—

All those double shifts pulled to pay for football cleats.

All those candles lit in church.

Everyone said Bobby wouldn't amount to anything.

BethAnn sighed.

An Excuse for a Baby

D o you need an excuse to want a baby? Typing this line out, I consider an alternative: "Does a *woman* need an excuse to want a baby?" But I reject this version because I've met men (admittedly, very few) who really wanted children, who spoke of the miracle of life, who spoke in the hyperbole of women. Because mostly, it *is* women—women who end up in short stories (stuff like this one) and novels and self-help books that should never have made it past an acquisitions editor. It's women who want babies.

But not all women. And that's where this question comes in. What about the "new woman"? The one with all those degrees and those test scores that put her in the percentile that used to make people (people? guidance counselors and admissions officers, really) talk of her limitless future and all her "potential"—and not babies. Like babies cancel out potential.

Or the "artist": the woman who didn't become a doctor or a lawyer but who took off in an RV for the West Texas desert . . . or, better yet, New Mexico. That girl. Who lived with the thirty-year-old skater and had the balls (she referred to balls intentionally—to be anti-feministly, post-something feminist) to call Kerouac out, the whole "that isn't writing; that's just typing" thing. What about her?

Does she have to explain, a week before her fortieth birthday, that yes, she supposes she would like a baby, that perhaps she has missed something . . . ? Asking aloud if there's still time . . . vexing the sister or best friend or yoga teacher unfortunate enough to have texted her about meeting for dinner tonight. Does she need an excuse to make it explicable?

"Yeah, the clock's ticking. Maybe I do . . . ."

"Maybe it would be nice. People talk about a new level of love when you hold them."

"I want to experience everything, and that's a big part of everything, you know?"

And perhaps even that ghastly "miracle of life."

No, she doesn't need an excuse. Or shouldn't need one. But she offers it anyway. Offers her age and accomplishments, her need for the "next adventure," her *creativity* . . . in all its forms . . . places them as holocausts on an alter God never intended for blood sacrifice.

*

His dog stopped, so he called out, asked those he could feel around him if the street was clear for him to cross. She glanced about and saw the green light, answered him that it was clear. She hadn't noticed the not-yet-frozen puddle ankle-deep in front of the curb.

Pianos and Silk Pajamas

My husband Michael has found an audience, which makes us both happy.

"They call it the Great Loop. It's a trip around the Eastern United States by boat," he explains to the young couple that has stopped on the dock to admire our trawler *Sojourn*. "We're from Houston. Came by way of the Intracoastal around Florida, up the East Coast, and through the Erie Canal."

"Wow," the woman says. She looks about thirty. "How long did it take?"

"Oh, we're taking our time," Michael replies. "We've been at it over two years now."

"She's really beautiful," the man says. "We have a Sea Ray, a Sundancer 260. Right over there." He gestures down the dock.

"Good boat to get started in," Michael lies. He hates Sea Rays and runs them and Carvers down every chance he gets.

"What's the fuel burn like on 'er?" the man asks Michael.

"Real economical. I don't open her up—no need—and we burn between three and four gallons an hour. And I'm still doing seven, eight knots at that.

"Nice," the man says.

"Would you like to take a look at her?" Michael gestures grandly from the deck and then walks aft toward the entryway in the rail. He opens the gate.

"Come aboard," he says. "Sweetheart," he calls to me, "have we got anything to share with—" He pauses.

"Victor," the man says, "Victor, and this is my wife Lilly. We're from Petoskey."

"I'm Michael Franks, and my wife is Elizabeth. Liza, where you gotten to, honey?"

"Right here. Right behind you," I answer, pushing *Sojourn*'s cabin door open and carrying out a tray of Chimays and an Aix Provence rosé.

"I've got a nice corn relish I'll bring right out, too," I say, stepping to the back deck and placing the tray on the little table we set out there when we made port in Harbor Springs. "I'm Elizabeth Franks." I offer my hand to Lilly, and then to Victor when he reaches me on the sundeck.

In the cabin, I reload the tray with corn-relish dip, water biscuits, a silver salver of truffles, and slices of sausage for Michael.

"Here we go." I return to the aft deck and set the tray beside the beer and wine. Michael has taken a seat beside the stern rail, and Victor and Lilly sit on either side of the table. Michael is telling them about how much we loved Mackinac Island.

"I'd never even heard of the place before I started researching this trip, but Liza knew about it. Knew it from that movie *Somewhere in Time*. With Christopher Reeve? You're from up here. You must know it."

"Oh, we know it." Victor reaches across the table and bats at Lilly's shoulder.

"I'm a bit of a sucker for pretty history," Lilly confesses. "I make him go to the island every year for the *Somewhere in Time* weekend at the Grand Hotel."

Michael laughs that West Texas Permian Basin laugh he likes to put on. "Sounds like Liza. She used to drag me all over the Gulf Coast for these piano events she'd do. She'd play at weddings and graduation parties and corporate events. Like we needed the money. But she loved it, I guess. She played all over and I chased around behind her, so she could do it."

I try to match his laugh. "We don't chase around for anything now."

"I'd love to be musical," Lilly says, "but I have no talent at all. I tried, too. I took piano lessons as a kid and guitar as an adult, but I just can't do it."

"You could," I assure her. "Anyone can—you just have to stick through the grind of it long enough to break through. It clicks for people at different times. Some people just have a knack for it. Some don't. But if you push through, anyone can get it."

"Push through and get a bigger boat and do the Loop," Michael says. "That's what you want to push through on. It's really the life. We don't worry about anything—life's slower. No worries."

He lifts the glass of Chimay to his lips.

"It seems just about perfect," Victor says. "You said her name's *Sojourn*?"

"Yep," Michael replies, "*Sojourn*. So lemme show you around."

He presses himself out of his chair, and Victor and Lilly follow him into the cabin. Through the windows, I can see him raise the cabin sole and display the twin Caterpillars. Over the stern rail, Lake Michigan glitters all cold and sharp, and the pebbly lakebed shows through beneath the boat's slip. On the teak railing, I tap out "Für Elise." The overhang from the upper deck absorbs summer and all that Northern Michigan sunshine, and I stand in its shade, and Beethoven gives way to Grieg. Behind me, the cabin door opens. I take a seat and pour another glass of rosé.

"So what do you think of a Grand Banks?" I ask.

"Oh, she's fantastic," Victor gushes. "She's real shippy. Nothing like the Sea Ray. I don't think we're ready for anything like this, but boy, she's beautiful."

"It's a lifestyle," Michael says. "You just gotta do it. Grab the bull by the horns and make your dreams come true. If you want it, it's yours." He bends over the table and dips a cracker into the relish dip.

"Victor would love to," Lilly says, taking her seat beside the table. "He'd go off into the sunset in an instant if we could afford it. But I think I'd miss too much . . . my mom and sister. We love to get together and go to Traverse City for shopping weekends. And I'd like to have kids. And I don't want to give up my career. At least not yet. Do you have children?"

"No," I reply. "I had a piano." I try to laugh. "But it's not the same thing."

She chuckles. "Don't you miss things?"

"Not a goddamn thing," Michael says. "Miss what? Traffic? Starbucks? If I want a good pull of espresso, I go in the cabin and get it." He laughs. "I don't miss a thing."

Lilly looks at me.

I laugh—and this time it works. "I miss silk pajamas. There's no place for them on a boat. But they sure were nice. To silk pajamas." I raise my glass.

Michael pours more beer into his glass. "We don't miss anything," he repeats. "This is the life."

"He assured me I'd love it," I say. "I remember our last night in our condo in Houston. We were having a sale the next day to sell off everything: the furniture and art and my Steinway. Michael said we'd move aboard the boat full time after that, and that we'd push off the dock as soon as all the accounts were in order. And we did."

I get up and step over to the table to retrieve a truffle.

"I remember wondering if I'd be happy doing this," I continue. "I got up in the middle of the night and went downstairs and played everything I could think of: Pachelbel and Debussy and Liszt and Scott Joplin and Coldplay. Everything. I didn't know when I'd get to play again. I felt like I just had to play."

"She played for hours," Michael says. "I woke up in the middle of the night to this music. I went downstairs and there she was in this blue silk nighty banging on those keys to save her soul." He shakes his head. "She had some music sittin' in front of her, but she wasn't readin' it. She had her eyes closed and I thought maybe she was sleep-playing." He laughs again. "We've had so many good times." And another shake of his head. "We don't miss a thing. Do we, honey? You miss that old piano? We've seen so much. We went to Hemingway's house in Key West and went over to the Bahamas. Spent a month there. Showed her Annapolis. I hadn't been back since my days at the Academy. Went to Fort Sumter, and she wanted to see all that shag dancing in Myrtle Beach, so we did that. Did all the history stuff in Philadelphia and D.C.—all those things we all say we'll do and never make time for, but boy, we've made the time, and it's a great life."

"Sounds amazing," Victor says, seeming somehow much younger than we are, though I think I have a decade on him at the very most.

"Don't get him started," Lilly says. "He's gonna be hell to live with after this."

"You haven't seen the bridge yet!" Michael rises suddenly. "Mea culpa."

He leads the way up the steps to the bridge, Victor dogging after him. Lilly trails. "It's romantic," she says to me as she steps by, "in theory, but I think I'd miss a lot."

"It's nice," I say. "You get used to it. You do."

"So when did you decide to do this?" Victor asks, coming down the stairs in front of Michael after Michael has cranked the Caterpillars and shown off their smooth starts and purr and the view from the upper deck.

"I've been planning this since I could read," Michael says. "When I was a kid, I read about Nat Palmer becoming the first American to discover Antarctica in the 1820s. I was hooked. I wanted to sail big boats on big seas and see the big world."

He throws his arms out and takes in Michigan and the Great Lakes and North America. "I went to Annapolis," he continues, "and then shipped out for six months and saw Rota—Spain—and Naples, and Alexandria. I knew I'd spend my life on the sea—I've had a boat of some size or shape ever since I left the Navy."

I excuse myself to find more wine in the cabin and return with a Joseph Phelps Insignia from Napa.

"That is amazing," Lilly says after she tastes it.

"2013," I respond. "They did all right in 2013." I grin.

"Did you dream of doing this, too?" she asks me. "Did you do boats before you met Michael?"

"To doing boats," I reply, raising my glass. We clink rims. "No, Ms. M/V *Sojourn* is all his. I like it, but it's not in my blood like it is for Michael." I take a sip of wine. "I've had hobbies, but I've never had Michael's deep passion for things." I look over at my husband. "Maybe I envy him that passion. You're a passionate man, honey."

He salutes me with his beer glass.

"To passion," he says.

We all raise our glasses.

"Where will you go after this?" Victor asks.

"Oh, we'll take our time working down Michigan and then spend some time in Chicago," Michael replies. "Then down the Mississippi to New Orleans. A lot of people go down the Tenn-Tom route, but I gotta do the Mississippi. Too much Tom Sawyer and Huck Finn in my childhood to pass that up. Then we'll head down the Texas coast to Port Isabel. Go into Mexico. I want to spend a couple months diving in Cozumel. That'll be nice."

Victor looks swept away. Michael leans forward and pours beer into Victor's empty glass.

"What's been the biggest highlight of your adventures so far?" Lilly asks.

"All of it," Michael says. "There ain't a day goes by that don't have a highlight."

I laugh. "There are ups and downs," I say. "But a big up was when we set out. We spent a night in Port Arthur, and we went to this bar. It was a bit run down, but there was a keyboard set up in a corner and I kept looking over my shoulder at it and Michael asked for the manager and gave him two hundred dollars to let me play. And I sat down at that keyboard and played for—how long, honey?"

"You kept them people going for hours, honey," Michael responds. "She started with 'Margaritaville' and everyone started clapping and she entertained them all night. People came up and tipped her and some people danced. She can really play."

"Not anymore." I shake my head.

"You've played since you were a kid?" Lilly asks.

"Yes, my mom was a piano teacher," I say. "The old 'blessing and a curse,' but it was mostly a blessing for me. She screamed—literally hopped around the house screaming, jumping from room to room— when I got accepted at Juilliard." I grin and drop my forehead into my hand, remembering my mum bouncing around like a bunny.

"You went to Juilliard?" Lilly lifts her glass and tilts it toward me. "And this is exquisite."

"Oh, she went to Juilliard," Michael answers, "and can sing, too."

"I'd love to hear," Lilly says.

"Oh, I haven't played in so long," I say, "since that night in Port Arthur actually. There's no place on a boat for a piano." I conjure that laugh. "Goes the way of the silk pajamas."

The beer supply has dwindled.

"I'll go get us some more." I gesture toward the bottles. "Chimay, honey? Or something else?"

Lilly gives Victor a look.

"We should be going," she says, rising from her seat.

"Yes," Victor agrees, "we've imposed enough. But thank you both so much for your hospitality and for sharing your boat and letting us see her. And for sharing your dream." He brushes a hand over Lilly's hair. "We're going to do this. You've convinced me. I'm going to make it happen."

Victor puts an arm around Lilly, and they take a step toward the gate in *Sojourn*'s railing.

"Our pleasure," Michael says. "Dreamers are always welcome aboard M/V *Sojourn*."

We see them off. They wave a last time when they reach the head of the dock. I carry the refreshment tray into the galley and wash up. Afterward, Michael pulls the sole up and descends into the engine room, and I track his progress by the sound of metal on metal and of masculine expulsions of breath. After he emerges from his jousting, he showers, carrying the orange bottle of Gojo soap up to the bathhouse with him, and when he returns, we walk through Harbor Springs in search of dinner and a few more drinks.

On the aft deck a couple hours later, we chase dinner and the dinner drinks with after-dinner drinks and I put Schumann on *Sojourn*'s stereo, Michael's marinized Bose speakers pouring "Arabesque" out onto the dusty-pink almost-night that has sidled up to the docks. Michael scoots his chair up to mine and drops an arm over my shoulders.

"We've made it to heaven and we didn't even have to die to do it, baby." He squeezes me.

I pat his knee.

In the berth that night, in my t-shirt and sweats that let me walk to the marina's bathhouse with impunity, I lay my head on his chest.

"I'm glad you're so happy," I whisper. "I love you."

"I love you too, babes. We're happy." He opens his eyes. "But I do miss your playin' sometimes."

*

My life was tinder, my volition a spark.
Lying and cheating and regretting until only springtime was left.

Honeymoon

They moved to Houston. Spent a year of dark nights climbing the fence surrounding NASA, their savings going for tools and bootlegged fuel. "I love you to the moon and back," she whispered to him the last night, as she closed the circuit and the old Saturn V rocket rumbled into lift off.

Anniversary

She did odd things, weird things, things other people wouldn't have understood. Took an Uber thirty-five minutes north to George Bush Intercontinental to stay at the Marriott there for one night every January 19th. Tipped everyone who served her in singles, explained that ones were the best bill. Bought her grandkids Curious George books long after they'd outgrown them, laughed it off when her daughter looked at her funny.

Nobody understood until an old man came to her funeral. Introduced himself as George. Said they'd met in high school, on January 19th, if he remembered right.

Mahogany Pilgrimage

If you want to restore a fifty-year-old wooden trawler, I recommend finding a warm place to do it. The Texas Gulf Coast works well: it's warm and affordable, and areas like those around Galveston Bay brim with shipyards, contractors, and marine resale shops. Clear Lake, Texas, southeast of Houston, boasts the third largest concentration of pleasure craft in the United States . . . however "they" define a measure for that. Even if you've grown up in Southern California and learned from a young age to snub the Texas side of the Gulf, you'll see the advantages of restoring an old boat here if you try it. In Kemah, you'll find boat slips for eight bucks a foot and a tourist boardwalk with an old wooden "bullet" roller coaster that has forty-two track crossovers built into it—the most of any wooden roller coaster ever designed. It's a place where people can live on boats berthed almost beneath the roller coaster and listen to the sound of teens shouting on wooden rails in the middle of thick summer nights.

Just a little north of Clear Lake and Kemah, you'll find Houston Yacht Club, and that's a nice place to keep an old wooden trawler because you don't have the roar of the coaster and you can put the old girl in a covered slip and keep the sun off her, which will save you on electric once you've installed marine air conditioning. But if you drive down to get your boat from someplace up north—say someplace nice and Rust Belt-y like Detroit or Gary, or Kalamazoo because then at least you've got a line in the history books about the Nicholas Brothers rocking to your town's World War II tune (and if you haven't seen that dance number, you should look it up on YouTube because it's very cool)—you'll appreciate the heat. You won't complain about the triple digits in the summer or the humidity you can carry in a bucket—because you know what it tastes like to blow snow in single-digit cold when you've got the flu and you can't pull the car in off the busy street you live on without first blowing the drive clear when you leave work early on sick time. Or the street you *lived* on. You don't live on it anymore. You looked at too many pictures of boats and beaches after blowing that snow, and you decided to chuck it all, and you put the cat in the car and left the job that gave you paid sick time, and drove to the Gulf Coast to find an old boat to bang your head against.

On Galveston Bay, you'll find lovely brown water. And around the bay, you'll find monuments that would likely make John Galt grin: some would say comely, some would say ghastly, imbroglios of oil-boiling machines lit in the night by flares of burning capital. If you drive down to the Island proper—Galveston Island—you'll see another monument: the one for the 1900 storm that may make you tear up a bit when you see the upward-reaching man—and his wife clutching their baby—and you realize 6,000 people died in that storm. Save some tears, though, for the drive home because you'll pass Texas City, where seventy-some years ago the U.S. experienced its largest industrial accident in history . . . an explosion of ships that started with ignition of a cargo of over 2,000 tons of ammonia nitrate. With over 8,000 victims, the Texas City disaster snuggled into a niche in legal history as launching the first class action against the U.S. government.

Find a palapa to sit under and have a drink and you'll think it was worth the trouble to get down here. A lot of places here have palapa bars, those thatched tropical structures under which girls in hotpants serve fireball drinks and local Texas beers like Shiner Bock and Elissa IPA, which is named for the tall ship at the Texas Seaport Museum on the Island, the Scottish barque christened for Carthage's Dido, the non-Virgil Dido . . . as other sources called her Elissa. If you sit under one of these palapas, even one on a busy highway with no view at all, you'll feel tropical, island-y, five-o'clock-somewhere-y.

If you've had the misfortune of becoming a vegetarian yoga teacher, your new-found lone-star friends will forgive you—as long as you don't espouse the idea of asking them to eschew the pleasures of animal flesh—or suggest that chili could be made of beans. The local massage therapist will appreciate your detailed anatomical descriptions of the pinch you're feeling in your piriformis, and then he'll ask you if you prefer handguns or long guns. He'll ask you about hunting because you mentioned that Rust Belt ex-home, and even in Texas, Michigan deer hunting shines supreme. He'll confess he's never field dressed a deer and you'll confess you have.

If you're serious about finding this boat, you'll use a yacht broker because they have access to tons more potential boats, and you're going to look at tons. It won't be easy to find your *Pilar*. Of course, you won't name her *Pilar* once you've found her, though you'll be sorely tempted to because you love Papa's stories and you loved Havana when you snuck over there a few years before Fidel died. But it would just be too cliché to borrow that name. You'll look at an old Beneteau raceboat, French and fast-ish and plastic. You'll pass on her and buy a little bluewater Pearson you and the cat can cruise together. The Pearson will be thirty-one feet long and have a nice shallow draft: less than four feet, so she can go all over Galveston Bay, which, in most places, isn't as deep as the pool at a lot of Ys. She'll be fiberglass, but that's okay right now. Together, the three of you (the boat, the cat, and you) will sail around to different marinas on Galveston Bay and live in the sun for a year and a half. You'll play cards at night with old men who won't admit that the wives who left them broke them, and you'll go to boat blessings for Canadian miners bound for the islands, and you'll knit sweaters (which you'll never be able to wear on the Gulf Coast) with women who cook Thanksgiving turkeys in propane-fueled, gimbaled ovens the size of shoeboxes.

For money, you'll write petitions to the U.S. Supreme Court for lawyers you knew before you had permanent sunburned flip-flop stripes across the tops of your feet. It won't be more than a couple grand a month in a good month, but you won't need much on that little boat. You'll fill the water tanks at night when it's not so hot, and brush your teeth with water from the sink, but you'll use the public bathhouse to shower. You'll eat dinners with cruisers down the dock, who mix drinks of rum from the local distillery and whatever juices Aldi has for sale that week. The storms will blow the water out of the marina and you'll see the big boats sitting at an angle, their keels dug in the mud when the water levels get really low.

People will talk about Ike—and now they will talk of Harvey—of the boats Ike blew into parking lots and impaled on posts, of boats wedged between trees and sunk in slips, of the marina where the worst damage was a torn genoa on a big cruising boat and of the marina off the ship channel where boats lay two hundred yards on shore with pieces of dock tied to their stern lines . . . left trailing across asphalt. With Harvey come the new stories, including the one in which your car floods and you bail her out, but the clutch rusts away and fails a month later. Or the one where the old steel ketch at anchor breaks loose and grinds ashore beside the Hilton near NASA and becomes the backdrop for pictures of teenagers heading back to school.

The security guard at the marina you're at for a couple months will tell you to keep the cat locked aboard the boat because the nine-foot alligator has been on the docks again. Or is it a crocodile? The water is brackish here, so you don't really know if it's a croc or a gator, but you think it's the latter. Maybe the cat will be black and white, a gift from an FBI agent you met outside the grand-jury room one afternoon when you were representing a dope dealer who was inside testifying. The agent did cat rescue and walked over to you and told you you needed a cat and you believed him, so now you have a cat who roams the docks and drops in people's hatches and watches TV with oldsters on Catalinas and Island Packets. It's really only the oldsters who care much about TV, dishes stuck to the bows of their boats, while the younger crowd walks in the evenings or plays card games or just drinks and tells stories that straddle the space between fish tales and lies.

When you go stand-up paddling at night, you think of that gator/croc on the dock and of his brothers and sisters, but you paddle across the channel to the bar where a duo plays Jimmy Buffet covers, and you stand on water in the night watching navigation lights twinkle, knowing you're somewhere better than Margaritaville, even though the highway through town is marked by dry brown lots (full of vehicles with "FOR SALE" in greasepaint on their windshields) and a strip club called the Double something. In the summer, the air feels like a favorite blanket, and it's those nights balanced on that board—mosquitos feasting on you—that make having no steady income and paying a bum-load for ObamaCare all worthwhile. In the winter, the mosquitos let you alone, but then the cold makes the air sharp and angular . . . like you could walk up it like stairs . . . and the water puts your bare feet to sleep. (At least it—the water—stays soft, though, unlike up north where you don't need a paddle board under you to walk on lakes in winter.)

You paddle out the channel to the bay, past the kids on the boardwalk who wave at you, past the lights of games of chance and alleged skill, past the bands playing eighties covers in front of the boardwalk hotel. You forget the tide and the Venturi effect where all that outbound water gets pinched up in the narrows under the bridge, and it's a lot harder to paddle home.

If you don't get writing work, you might try to sell boats for the same brokerage that sold you the Pearson. The local marine surveyor will meet you at boats for survey, showing up on a jet ski he's ridden over from the marina where he lives. The woman at the shipyard always gets you time on the travel lift to haul boats out to show off to prospective buyers. The workers will joke with you in Spanish after you make a smart-ass remark about knowing what they're saying about the *güera*. They zip into Tyvek suits to sand fiberglass on sport-fishing boats and paint sailboat hulls the color of the sky. The men work in the relentless summer, and the woman in the office rides past them in a golf cart to force them to drink water from bottles she hands out. She may complain to you about the inconvenience of workers passing out in the heat. The sun darkens the men to match the tooled belts they'll wear to the Rumba Club in the evening to dance *bachata* and salsa and listen to reggaeton over weak drinks with black-haired women.

When enough writing work comes in or you sell a boat, you might go to the pho place in Kemah. People say the pho is so good here because of the shrimping industry, which allegedly attracted Vietnamese fishermen who outcompeted most others. Locals explain the quality of the pastries by citing French colonial rule in Vietnam, which has supposedly left its mark in Texas in little spongy, colored treats extolled on table tents. If you don't get pho, you might go to the biker place in San Leon that won't take anything but cash and won't welcome kids. They have good boudain, though that may not matter to you because you may yet be refusing to give up the vegetarianism. Or there's the oyster place down there with all those marble-white oysters from the Gulf that people fork onto saltine crackers and top with cocktail sauce and horseradish and slide down their throats on slip 'n slides of beer.

That place (the oyster place) has the wooden gliders outside where you can sit under canvas sunshades and rock back and forth as you eat what's been caught from the waters essentially in front of you. A concrete dock welcomes boats with drafts shallow enough to nose up to it, and men with one hundred fifty horses behind them will outrun their wakes to pull up and order beer. You, on the other hand, may have gotten there on the back of a Harley, hanging on behind a seventy-year-old who circled the globe with a jury-rigged forestay and a shipboard bathtub decorated with tiny reflective mosaic tiles that do nothing but make the head look fancy.

From those gliders outside the restaurant or from the marina pavilion or from the yacht-club clubhouse, or looking up from the old Pearson's cockpit at night, the world may look prettier, even when you're lonely or you need new brakes and you can't afford them. (Never do you get to complain about such circumstances because you chose them. You always felt a little contempt toward Kerouac complaining about the road—he chose his adventure—so you know enough not to complain.) Everything simply looks prettier. Everything seems easier when all that you own fits inside thirty-one feet of fiberglass, when carpet feels like sheer luxury and ice is a treat. So Galveston Bay is a good place to fix up a boat.

This ease may make you cocky. You may remember Dana's *Two Years Before the Mast* and the romance of "iron men in wooden boats." That Beneteau you didn't buy—the one you looked at when you first drove down here from somewhere up north you barely remember—she belonged to a fellow you may later meet on match.com, perhaps a year later. And maybe a year after that you'll marry him—because you both love boats and you both love that seam between sea and sky with its stitches just loose enough for a little boat to slip through. Then together you'll find her: *Peregrine*, a little mahogany *peregrina* left in a shipyard by an old man struck by cancer. The yard has her title and wants only a bit of what they put into her on credit before the old man sailed over the bar.

In the yard, you'll put new decks on her. You'll be sad to see the teak go, but it's fifty years old and rotten through. You may decide to settle for fiberglass because if you're both going to live on her you will likely want to be dry. The old Pearson leaked and the cat would track through the puddles and everything would be wet during the heavy rains, and the cat would look at you and accuse you, and you can't take that level of accusation again. So *Peregrine* needs to be dry.

Plumbing and marine air conditioning may come next. Then you move aboard, and it's the first time you've lived aboard with someone besides the cat. She (the cat) comes too, and she remembers how to swim—she used to jump off the stern of the Pearson and swim to the dock, and you'd have to wash her because the water has diesel and discharge and other things in it that you wouldn't want the cat licking off her fur. The next pilgrimage begins, and you're glad to start it someplace warm.

Acknowledgments

A short-story collection does not spring from the brow of a Zeus-like book god fully formed—like some literary Minerva (feel free to substitute Athena or Jupiter if the mixing of Greek and Roman makes your skin crawl). The birth of *L*ve & Other Misunderstandings* involved the care, passion, support, and . . . well . . . love (without the asterisk) of more faithful "midwives" than I can name. And the book rests on the friendship, misadventures, anecdotes, and reflections of a veritable Roman legion. But I do want to thank, in a special ("official") way, Robyn Kelly for her editorial support, Stony James for his insight and literary sense of humor that laid fiberglass on a couple key stringers, Matthew Freeman for a summer in Michigan, Katelin Cummins for her confidence in "the process," and SLM for everything else . . . and Elizabeth Sterling, Melody Corkill Reynolds, Steve Barry, Tom Loftis, Paul and Lisa Stehfest, and Kerri Wenum for sheets snugged home.

Publication & Award Credits

A few of these pieces enjoyed life in print before appearing in this collection. Some have received awards.

"St. Peter's Salsa Club" appeared in Kallisto Gaia Press's *The Ocotillo Review* 3.2 (2019);

"Francis Roy Winters, Esq., Dives Off a Dock" appeared in Kallisto Gaia Press's *The Ocotillo Review* 3.1 (2019) (short-listed for the 2018 Chester B. Himes Memorial Short Fiction Prize);

"Queen" appeared in HWG Press's anthology *Outside the Window* (2018) and in the *Birmingham Arts Journal* 15.1 (2018) (first place in the Houston Writers Guild 2017 Short-Story Contest and second place in the Hackney Literary Awards 2017 National Story Contest);

"Milwaukee" appeared in HWG Press's anthology *Outside the Window* (2018) (honorable-mention status in the Houston Writers Guild 2017 Short-Story Contest);

"Dispute" appeared on the U.K.-based *Wild Words* electronic platforms (2018) (overall winner of the *Wild Words* Winter Solstice Competition 2017);

"Rings" received semi-finalist recognition for *Ruminate Magazine*'s 2018 William Van Dyke Short Story Prize;

and

"Mahogany Pilgrimage" received honorable-mention status in the *Flyway: Journal of Writing & Environment* 2017 Notes from the Field Creative-Nonfiction Contest.

About Sage Webb

Sage Webb practiced criminal defense for over a decade before turning to fiction. She is the author of two novels (*The Unremarkable Circumstances of Inmate 17656-090*, released by Martin Brown in 2018, and *The Venturi Effect*, forthcoming from Stoneman House Press in 2020). Her literary awards include second place in the 2017 Hackney Literary Awards and Red City Review's 2018 Best Debut Novel Prize. In 2020, Michigan's Mackinac State Historic Parks named her an artist in residence. She belongs to International Thriller Writers and PEN America, and lives with her husband, a ship's cat, and a boat dog on a sailboat in Galveston Bay.

You can find her at www.sagewebb.com.

If you enjoy her work, she always appreciates a review on your favorite book-purchasing platform.

Stoneman House Press

Stoneman House Press, L.L.C., prides itself on publishing books that blur boundaries, raise questions, and keep readers up late into the night: intelligent, original, and unexpected. Find your next favorite read at www.stonemanhouse.com.

Read Local

Read Local® offers an online community dedicated to the works of independent presses, with book reviews and thoughts on things literary, local, small, and funky. Join the discussion at www.readlocalbooks.org